GLORY DUST

Chaney Brothers 1

ROBERT VAUGHAN

WOLFPACK
PUBLISHING
—— EST 2018 ——

Paperback Edition
Copyright © 2019 Robert Vaughan

Published in the United States by Wolfpack Publishing, Las Vegas

Wolfpack Publishing
6032 Wheat Penny Avenue
Las Vegas, NV 89122

wolfpackpublishing.com

Paperback ISBN 978-1-64119-747-2
eBook ISBN 978-1-62918-906-2

Library of Congress Control Number: 2019947817

GLORY DUST

CHAPTER 1

April 1865 near New Madrid, Missouri

UNDER A CLUSTER OF TREES NEAR THE wagon road, a group of horsemen waited. They were Southern soldiers, though after four years of war they no longer had uniforms to wear. The grand gray and gold uniforms which they once wore so proudly had long since been replaced by denim and butternut. It didn't matter, for even if these men had been wearing uniforms no one could tell because they were all wearing oil slickers and wide-brimmed hats to keep out the rain. The wagon road by which they were waiting was covered with water and flushed with black mud, evidence of the rich delta swampland of southeast Missouri.

One of the horsemen, Clay Beekman, stood in his stirrups, scratched his crotch, then settled back again. He looked toward his leader.

"Cap'n Chaney, if you was to ask me, I don't think they'll be comin' out in this kind of weather," Clay said. He squirted a stream of tobacco juice toward a mud puddle where it swirled brown for a moment, then was quickly washed away.

Buck Chaney took off his hat and poured water from the brim, then put it back on to cover his wet blond hair. He reached down and patted his horse soothingly. He looked at Clay through gunmetal gray eyes which were alert and sparkling, despite the rain.

"They'll come," he said. "General Wilson is in Sikeston waiting for the gold they're carrying. He intends to put it on a train and take it over to the river, then put it on a boat to St. Louis. They're going to give the money back to the Yankee government in Jefferson City."

"Well, even if they do come, what makes you think they'll be comin' up this road?" Clay's brother, Carl, asked.

"Because this is the only road," Buck explained easily. "Everything else around here is swamp."

"They might go through the swamp," Carl suggested.

Buck laughed. "They're shipping the gold in strongboxes. Nine-hundred-thousand dollars' worth of gold weighs over four-hundred pounds. They'll put that on a wagon, and that means they'll be using this road."

"Cap'n, I hear 'em," one of the others said, and Buck held up his arm to call for silence. Then, through the rain, he could hear the driver whistling and shouting at his team to urge them on.

"Deekus, you got your tree notched?"

"Yes, sir. All it'll take is about two whacks, and it'll drop right across that road, clean as a whistle."

"What about behind 'em, Cap'n?" Clay asked.

"Don't worry about that. They can't get the wagon turned around on this road. The tree will keep them from going forward and we'll keep them from going back."

"Hell, if you ask me, we ought to just shoot the sons of bitches. They're all Yankees anyhow."

"We'll do it my way, Beekman," Buck said. "Now, get into position."

The men melted back into the woods and waited as the wagon and its escort detail came up the road. Buck, who had been raised in this part of southeast Missouri, knew the country like the back of his hand. He knew that this was the best place between New Madrid and Sikeston to set up the ambush, because the road here was so muddy as to be nearly impassable.

From the shouts and whistles, Buck knew that the driver was having to work the team exceptionally hard. A moment later they came into view and Buck could see the horses straining to pull the wagon through the mud.

With an eye trained by four years of military ambushes, Buck looked at how the detail was deployed. Four of the soldiers were riding in front of the wagon, there were two on the wagon—the driver and an armed guard—and there were four more soldiers behind the wagon. The officer-in-charge was riding between the four lead soldiers and the wagon.

The rain was falling so hard that visibility was limited to a few hundred feet and for the moment that was decidedly to Buck's advantage. His men were hidden in the trees, completely out of sight, whereas the Union soldiers were on the road, in plain view.

Buck held his hand up, preparatory to giving the signal, when, unexpectedly, the detail stopped. The officer-in-charge rode to the front of the detail, stopped, then looked down the road.

"Well," Buck mused quietly. "You're smarter than I thought you were, Yankee. You know this is the only place you can be ambushed, don't you?"

The officer-in-charge sent two of his soldiers down the road ahead of them and Buck turned to make certain that his men were well concealed. He motioned for Deekus, who was standing by his notched tree, to get out of sight. At his signal, Deekus slipped back into the woods.

If the soldiers who rode ahead had been more

observant, the officer-in-charge might have been forewarned. There were some freshly cut wood chips floating in the water on the road, put there from the notching of the tree, but the point-riders didn't notice them. Even the notch itself could have been seen if they had looked, but they didn't look. They were interested only in keeping their collars turned up and their hat brims turned down to keep out as much of the cold spring rain as possible. They were humoring their commander by riding down the road for what, to them, was just a waste of time.

The Union soldiers weren't thinking of any possible danger facing them. They thought only of the dry barracks they would find when they reached their camp in Sikeston. They rode at a canter through the narrow, muddiest part of the road, then they turned their horses and went back, reporting to the commander that all was well.

The officer-in-charge, who was a major, sat on his horse for a long moment, as if contemplating the report. For a moment, Buck had an idea that the Yankee major didn't believe his men, and was going to check out the road for himself.

"You've got a hunch, don't you, Yankee?" Buck whispered under his breath.

Finally, the Yankee major gave the order to proceed.

With a sigh of relief, Buck signaled for Deekus

to return to his position by the tree, and he stood there watching the Yankees come ahead, waiting until the detail was committed.

At the appropriate time Buck brought his hand down. There were two sharp reports as the axe took the final two bites from the towering cypress tree. With groans, creaks, and loud snapping noises, the tree started down, then fell across the muddy road with the crashing thunder of an artillery barrage. At the same time the tree hit the road in front of the Union detail, Buck's men moved out onto the road behind them and fired several shots into the air.

"You're surrounded!" Buck shouted, urging his horse onto the road from the trees right alongside. He leveled his pistol at the Union soldiers. "Throw up your hands."

The Union soldiers were quick to throw down their rifles, but the major brought his own pistol from beneath his poncho and pointed it at Buck, then pulled the trigger. Buck saw the cylinder turn and heard the hammer click, but the cartridge misfired. Buck aimed at the major and started to fire, when he suddenly recognized a man he hadn't seen in over four years. He withheld his fire.

"Lance! Lance, drop your gun! For God's sake, don't make me shoot you!" Buck shouted anxiously.

The Union officer, surprised to be addressed by name, peered through the rain at Buck, then, recognition showed in his face as well. He lowered his gun and let it drop into the mud.

"Buck?" he said. "Buck, is that you?"

"You know this Reb, Major?" one of his soldiers asked.

"Yes, I know him," Lance answered. Then, to Buck, he said, "So, after all these years, we finally meet across the lines."

Buck signaled the rest of his men to come forward. "I've come to relieve you of your burden," Buck said. "Do you have the keys to the strongboxes?"

"No," Lance answered.

"No matter. We can take care of that. Clay?"

Clay shot the locks off the boxes, one at a time, then let out a little shout of joy when the first bag was produced. Deekus brought up a pack mule and he and the Beekman brothers started loading the gold dust into the mule's saddlebags.

Lance twisted around on his horse to watch the loading.

"Buck, if you take that gold, you know I'm going to have to come after it," he said. "And that means I'll be coming after you."

"Haw!" one of the Beekmans laughed. "You ain't goin' to get too far with lead in your ass. We aim to shoot ever' damn one of you Yankee bastards."

"You'd better shoot me now," Lance replied quietly. "Because if I ever see you again, it's going to be from the other side of the gun."

"We're not going to shoot you," Buck said.

"Am I supposed to be grateful for that? What if it had been another officer in charge of this detail? An officer you didn't know. Would you have shot him?" Lance asked.

"Not unless it was necessary," Buck answered. "Come on, Cap'n, you know we can't take no prisoners," Clay Beekman protested.

"We aren't taking prisoners," Buck said. "But we aren't killing them, either."

"Then what are we going to do with 'em?" Clay asked.

"You let me worry about that."

"I think your man has a good point, Buck," Lance said. "Just what do you plan to do with us?"

Buck looked at him for a moment, then he smiled. "Tell me, Lance, are you fellows wearin' some of those nice, warm, Yankee long johns right now?"

"Why do you ask?"

"I just don't want you catching a fever when I leave you here, that's all."

"Buck! Wait a minute, Buck. If you're thinking what I think you're thinking, you're crazy!" Lance said.

Buck laughed. "I'm not crazy. I'm just a man with

a long memory is all. I seem to recall you leaving me stranded out on Wolf Island once," he replied. "You took the boat and my clothes and left me there till I could hail a passing flatboat."

"We were kids," Lance said. "That was a joke."

"Yeah, well, so's this," Buck said. "Now, shuck out of your clothes. All of you."

"Now, just you fellows wait a minute!" one of the Union soldiers said. "I ain't goin' to do nothin' of the kind."

"You heard the cap'n, Blue-belly," one of Buck's men said, laughing. He made a signal with his carbine. "Get out of 'em."

The soldiers grumbled and protested, but a few minutes later all eleven of them, including Lance, were standing in the mud in their long johns. Their uniforms were on the back of Buck's pack mule.

"Clay, get their horses. Carl, you and Deekus tie our Yankee friends to the wagon."

"That won't do no good, Cap'n," Deekus said. "Why, in this rain they'll slip out of the ties in no time."

"It'll give us time to get away," Buck said. "And without clothes or horses, they won't be able to catch up to us."

"Oh, I'll catch up with you, all right," Lance said, angrily. "I promise you that, Buck. I'll catch you, and I'll get every ounce of that gold back."

"That's big talk, Blue-belly, from a man who's standing here tied to a wagon, nigh-on-to naked," one of Buck's men said, and they all laughed at the plight of the Yankee soldiers.

"Let's go," Buck ordered, and he and his men started away at a gallop.

"I'll get you, Buck!" Lance shouted at him. "I'll get you for this, if it's the last thing I do!"

It only took ten minutes for Lance and his men to work their way out of the ropes, but Lance knew that Buck was right. It was too late then to do anything about recovering the gold. Lance thought of General Wilson and the others who were expecting him. He wasn't looking forward to the reception that would be waiting for them when they got back to Sikeston, but he had no choice. He had to go and report what had happened. When he looked around at his men he saw that they were all standing around in utter confusion. Despite himself, Lance couldn't help but laugh a short, bitter laugh, at the sight of them.

Lance had seen over four years of war and had fought battles at Belmont, Shiloh, Fredericksburg, Vicksburg, Lookout Mountain, and Franklin. But not one man on this detail had ever heard a shot fired in anger, or even seen a Rebel in the field until a few moments ago. They were all new recruits, doing garrison duty in a backwater town, in a place where most of the fighting was already over, marking time until the final collapse of the rebellion.

When Lance was given the assignment to transport the gold he knew that such a prize might lure an attack from one of the few guerrilla bands remaining in the area. Because of that he asked for a detail composed of veterans, but his request was turned down.

Perhaps if Lance had been given what he asked for he could have prevented the loss. At the very least, he could have expected them to put up a fight and not just throw down their weapons as these men had done. He thought of the men who had fought with him at Shiloh. When he compared these men with those, his present command did not come off very favorably.

Already these men were talking about the "close call" they just had, and he knew that many of them were actually excited by their brush, no matter how lightly, with the war. He sighed. There was only one thing to do now, and that was get them back to Sikeston.

"All right, men, fall in," he commanded.

"Fall in? Well, what is it you are aimin' for us to do, major?"

"We're going back to Sikeston," Lance informed them.

"How we goin' back? We ain't got no mounts."

"We'll march."

"You aim to walk us all the way there?"

"It's only eleven miles," Lance offered. "That's just a stroll to the infantry."

"But we ain't infantry, Major. We're cavalry," one of the men protested.

"Oh, you're cavalry, are you?" Lance teased. "Then tell me, trooper, where's your horse?"

The others laughed at Lance's remark.

"The only horse you're goin' to be ridin', Johnson, is 'shank's mare,'" someone else said, and that, too, brought laughter.

Lance smiled. Maybe this wasn't as poor a lot as he thought. If they could laugh at their situation now, instead of grumble, they might be all right.

"Let's go, men," he said, and, in marching order, they began sloshing through the mud toward Sikeston.

They made a strange sight when they came into town a few hours later, covered with mud and marching in formation as if on parade drill, though dressed only in their long johns.

Many of the citizens of Sikeston were Southern sympathizers and they got a great enjoyment out of seeing the Yankee soldiers coming to town in such a condition. They knew it could only mean that they had encountered Confederate soldiers, and had obviously lost the engagement. The good citizens stood in front of their houses and in the doors of the stores and saloons, and they laughed and hooted at Lance and his men.

"What kind of company you got there, Major?" someone shouted. "Is that the new Yankee uniform?"

"You remember the Zouaves?" another asked. "Well, this is like the Zouaves, only they call this the Underwear Brigade."

"No, no! The Pantaloon Dragoons!"

The comments were met with more laughter.

"You wait till I—" one of Lance's men started to reply, but Lance cut him short.

"You're in formation, mister. No talking!" Lance hissed, sharply.

Looking neither left nor right and fuming silently under the cruel and ceaseless ribbing, Lance's men marched in parade step up King Street to the Cairo and Fulton railroad depot where General Wilson was waiting for Lance. Lance brought his detail to a halt, then saluted the general.

"I expect you'd better come inside, Major," General Wilson said, and Lance dismissed his men, then followed the general into the station house where the general had made his headquarters. Someone gave Lance a blanket and General Wilson poured him a glass of whiskey. Lance accepted both with thanks, then sat down when the general indicated that he should do so.

"I suppose the big question is, where's the gold?" General Wilson asked.

"It's gone, General," Lance said. "We were attacked right in the middle of the swamp. They dropped a tree across the road in front of us, then came onto the road behind us."

"How many casualties?"

"No casualties," Lance answered. "There was no fight."

The general looked surprised. "Let me get this straight, Major. You let the Rebels take nine-hundred- thousand dollars away from you and you didn't even put up a fight?"

Lance could have told the general that his green soldiers threw their weapons in the mud at the first sight of the enemy. He could have reminded him, also, that he had requested veterans for this detail. But that would have been transferring the blame, and he wouldn't do that. Lance had been the commander. That meant the blame was his and he was willing to shoulder it.

"No, sir," he said. "There was no fight."

"Damnation!" General Wilson swore. He slammed his hand down on the table in front of him, then got up and walked over to stand beside the little wood- burning stove which was now popping and snapping with a good fire. The general held his hands out over the stove for a few minutes to catch the warmth, then he looked back at Lance.

"Do you have any idea where they may have come from? I didn't know there were any large Confederate units still operating in this part of the country."

"They were guerrillas, sir," Lance said. "They were with Colonel Armstrong's Raiders."

"Armstrong?"

"Yes, sir."

"Armstrong, Thompson, Quantrill, Anderson, and all those other so-called guerrillas are little more than criminals. There's going to be some settling up to do with people like them one of these days. By the way, how do you know these men were with Armstrong?" Lance took the final swallow of his whiskey, then put the glass down and wiped the back of his hand across his mouth.

"I know, because I recognized the man who led the party," he said. "It was Buck Chaney."

"Did you say his name was Chaney?" General Wilson asked, looking at Lance in surprise.

"Yes, sir," Lance answered. "Same as mine. Buck Chaney is my brother."

CHAPTER 2

BUCK AND HIS MEN HEADED SOUTH ON the road known as El Camino Real. By now the rain had stopped but the sky was still overcast. The clouds were low-hanging and snagged by the upper branches of the towering trees that formed an almost impenetrable wall down either side of the road. Snake doctors darted about the cypress trees which stood waist-high in the swamp water, and great bullfrogs thrummed as the small band of raiders passed by.

Buck had planned to take the money from the strongboxes then make a hasty retreat to the south, but the pack mule had other ideas. Despite Buck's urging, the mule wasn't willing to go any faster than a quick walk. Buck had taken personal responsibility for the mule and he stayed back with the animal while his men rode on, several yards ahead of him.

The men were anxious because they were in territory controlled by the enemy, and as they rode, they were gradually opening the gap between them and Buck. Buck was also concerned about Yankee patrols, so he ordered Deekus to go ahead of the party to scout the road. Deekus had been gone about half-an-hour when Clay and Carl Beekman turned and rode back to Buck.

"Cap'n, can't you make that critter move any faster? We got to get out of here," Clay urged. "We can't be spendin' the rest of the day hangin' around on this road."

"Tell our friend that," Buck said, tugging on the mule's lead. "He won't listen to me."

"Hell, why don't we just shoot the son of a bitch and divide up the gold amongst us?" Carl suggested.

"You'd like that, wouldn't you, Carl?" Buck replied. "Yeah, you and your brother would both like that."

"What are you talkin' about?"

"If I gave you and your brother a bag of gold apiece, the South would never see you nor the gold again," Buck said.

"Cap'n, you got no right to say that 'bout Carl and me," Clay put in quickly. "We're loyal Confederates, both of us. Me'n him's fought this whole war for the South."

"Oh, I know. You're Jeff Davis's finest," Buck said, sarcastically.

"Damn right we are," Carl replied. "We've been in on this fight right from the very beginnin'."

"Yeah, I know how you've been in on it," Buck said. "To the two of you the war's been nothing but one big plunder...you knock over a bank in Bloomfield or pull a raid in New Madrid and say you're fighting for the South. But I didn't see you at Columbus, or Fort Donnelson, or Shiloh, or Vicksburg. While good men, in gray and blue, were dying in those battles, you two were robbing stagecoaches and pocketing most of the money."

"What money we kept was no more than fair, Cap'n," Clay defended. "Anyway, who are you to talk? You might've fought in all them battles you're talkin' about, but you're with us now. And this wasn't exactly no big battle we just had. This here ain't no different from what me and Carl's been doin' all along, only there's more money is all."

"But there is a difference," Buck said. "A big difference."

"Yeah? Well, I'm damned if I can see what it is."

"Money you take from a bank, or a stage, is private money, and people are hurt by it. This money belongs to the government of the state of Missouri, the true government, not the one the Yankees put in charge. I intend to see that it gets in the right hands."

They heard an approaching horse and looked up

to see Deekus coming toward them at a full gallop.

"Cap'n! Cap'n, Yankees!" Deekus shouted. "They's Yankees no more'n a mile behind me!"

"Are they coming this way?"

"Yes, sir. 'Bout fifty of 'em, I'd say. And they're comin' lickety split. They'll be here in no more'n two or three minutes."

"Damn!" Buck said. He took off his hat, ran his hand through his wet hair, and looked at the stubborn mule he was leading. He sighed. "All right," he finally said. "Deekus, there's a road leading west about a quarter of a mile back. Do you remember it?"

"Yes, sir," Deekus answered.

"I'm going back there to take that road. I can't make this mule go any faster than he's been going, so you're going to have to create a diversion to give me time to get away. I want you to get the men off the road, out of sight. When the Yankee patrol gets here, open fire on them."

Deekus spit out a stream of tobacco, then wiped the back of his hand across his mouth. Deekus was a sergeant who had been with Buck in all the battles Buck had mentioned. In fact, of Buck's original company, only Deekus and two other men remained. All others had fallen in battle. Buck had been in the regular army fighting under General Pemberton until the fall of Vicksburg. Then, with

Pemberton's army defeated, Buck and the few men left to him joined Colonel Armstrong's Raiders. Guerrilla companies such as Armstrong's Raiders were just about the only Southern forces in this part of the country now and anyone who wanted to continue the war had to do so in such units.

"I reckon I can do that for you, Cap'n," Deekus said.

"Cap'n Chaney, you don't intend for us to take on the whole Yankee army, do you?" Clay asked. "Deekus said they was fifty or more of 'em."

"Yes, and I doubt that more than five of them have ever heard a shot fired in anger," Buck said. "All the Yankee troops here are green now, you know that. When Grant went east to fight Lee, he took his veterans with him. You'll have good cover in the swamp; it won't take much to completely demoralize them."

"I still don't like it," Clay complained.

"You gotta take into account, Cap'n, that the Beekmans here, ain't all that used to fightin' against folks that fight back," Deekus said.

Clay and Carl Beekman glared at Deekus.

"Get them in position," Buck said. "We'll meet in Colonel Armstrong's camp." Buck started back as he called out the last sentence to Deekus, and by now he could hear the jangle of equipment and the drumming of hoofbeats as the large Yankee patrol came closer. Fortunately, there was a bend in the road just ahead and Buck figured to be around it and out of sight of the Yankees by the time they arrived.

"All right, men, off the road!" he heard Deekus order.

Buck was not only around the bend, he made it as far as the road by the time he heard the shooting begin. He didn't feel anxious for his men...Deekus was more than able to handle the situation and if he could choose right now, he would much rather be one of the ambushers than the ambushed. All the advantages: cover, surprise, and concealment, were with the Rebels who were waiting in the swamp for the unsuspecting Yankee patrol.

The mule, which had steadfastly refused to move faster than a walk, was frightened by the gunfire, and he suddenly began to run. As a result of that, Buck managed to cover two miles in about ten minutes. Two miles was all he needed, because that brought him to Doubletree Farm.

Buck stopped at the gate that led onto the farm and looked at the sign which hung from an old, weather- polished doubletree.

DOUBLETREE FARM
Roy Chaney and Sons

Roy Chaney had died in the first year of the war. The doctor said it was dropsy. Others said it was of a heart broken by the fact that his two sons had chosen opposite sides in the war. The mother died the next year and now only Becky and the boys' Aunt Ella remained behind. Becky was Buck and Lance's younger sister.

Buck stopped at the barn and took the bags of gold off the mules back. He raised a loose board in the floor of the barn and, as quickly as he could, tossed the bags under it. When all the bags were under the floor he replaced the loose board then moved hay over it to conceal the hiding place. He took the harness and packsaddle off the mule, then turned it loose and the mule, thankful to be free of its burden, brayed, shook its head, then ran out of the barn and into the pasture. Buck fed his horse, then walked from the barn up to the house.

"Unless you want a bullet between your eyes, mister, you've come far enough," a young woman's clear, strong voice called from the back of the house.

"Becky! Becky, it's me, Buck!"

"Buck? Is it really you?"

"Do you know anyone else this ugly?" Buck called back.

There was a squeal of delight, then a young woman burst through the back door and ran down the path toward Buck. She had her arms spread wide and Buck grabbed her in an embrace, then swung her around once, laughing and squeezing her affectionately.

Though Buck had been back in southern Missouri and northern Arkansas for nearly a year now, this was the first time he had come home. In fact, this was the first time he had seen Becky in almost four years. He had purposely avoided coming around, because he was afraid that the Yankees might be keeping an eye on the house. Like every other member of Colonel Armstrong's Raiders, Buck was a man with a price on his head. The Yankees had let it be known that they didn't consider guerrillas as legitimate soldiers...and sometimes Buck agreed with them.

Buck held Becky at arm's length and looked at her. He let out a low whistle.

"My God, look at you," he said. "You've grown into a woman. A beautiful woman!"

Becky smiled, proudly. "I'm eighteen now," she said. "That's full grown, in case you didn't know." Buck heard a sound from the back of the house, and his reflexes, honed sharp by four years of survival, took over. His pistol was in his hand in an instant, and he peered toward the back porch with narrowed eyes. Quickly, Becky put her hand on his arm.

"No," she gasped. "Buck, it's only Duke."

Buck smiled, and put the pistol back in his holster. Duke was an old black man who had been with the family for years. Buck's father had bought Duke as a slave, but, even before the war, he had freed his slaves. Many, like Duke, stayed on, either not able to understand their freedom, or unable to take advantage of it. It had been Duke who taught Buck and Lance how to fish and hunt.

"Mr. Buck? Mr. Buck, is that you?" Duke called. He moved toward Buck to embrace him.

"Duke, you're still here?"

"Yes, sir, I still be here," Duke said, smiling broadly. "This here be my home. Where else would I go?"

"I don't know what Aunt Ella and I would do without him," Becky said. "He's taken care of us ever since mama died."

"'Course, Mr. Lance, he be down here ever so often," Duke put in quickly. "He's been awful good 'bout bringin' us things we need. Do Mr. Lance be with you now?"

"I'm afraid not," Buck said.

"That purely be a shame," Duke said. "It'll be a mighty happy day 'round here, the day I see you two together again like brothers ought to be."

Buck laughed. "I don't think it would be a good idea for Lance and me to be together just now," he said.

"Buck, how long can you stay?" Becky asked.

"Not long, no more than a couple of minutes I'm afraid, then I'll have to be on my way. This is dangerous territory for me."

"You can stay to supper, can't you?"

"I'd better not," Buck said.

"Are you sure? I'll have Aunt Ella fry a chicken." Aunt Ella had been Roy Chaney's sister. When her own husband died twenty years ago, she came to Doubletree Farm to get over her grief, and she stayed. She had never made herself a burden though. On the contrary, she had helped cook and keep house, and had been good company for Sarah Chaney. And Aunt Ella's fried chicken had always been a particular favorite of Buck's. Just the thought of it made his mouth water. He smiled at Becky.

"All right, I'll stay," he agreed. "But just for supper."

"Aunt Ella, I do believe this is the best chicken I've ever eaten," Buck said half an hour later, as he started on his third piece.

"You're just saying that 'cause it's been a while since you had any," Aunt Ella replied, though it was obvious she was pleased by his comment. She took a pan of biscuits from the oven and lifted two of them out, then put them on Buck's plate. Buck opened the steaming hot biscuits and covered them with butter and honey.

"They say the war's nearly over," Becky suggested.

"I suspect it is," Buck replied. He sighed, then held the biscuit away from his mouth for a moment. "The truth is, it was over for the South when we lost Vicksburg and Gettysburg in the same week."

"Yet you continued to fight," Becky said. "Why?"

"You don't abandon honor, just because you lose on the battlefield," Buck said.

"Lance is fighting just as hard for honor, but from the opposite side of the question," Becky pointed out. "Does that mean one of you is with honor and the other is without?"

"No," Buck said. "Honor isn't determined by the question. Honor is determined by men's reaction to the question. I respect Lance for doing what he believes in...and I hope he respects me." Suddenly, and unexpectedly, Buck chuckled. "After today, though, he may have a different opinion."

"Why? What happened today?"

Buck told about his encounter with Lance. He didn't tell Becky about the gold, but he did tell her about leaving Lance and his men tied up in their long johns.

Becky laughed. "He'll never forgive you for that, Buck. Not in a hundred years."

Buck finished the biscuit. "It serves him right," he said. "He did the same thing to me on Wolf Island."

"Yes, but you were kids. To leave him like that now," Becky said. She laughed again. "But I have to admit, I would liked to have seen him. I'll bet it was funny."

"Miss Becky, Mr. Buck, they's horses comin'," Duke said, stepping into the dining room at that moment.

"I've got to get out of here," Buck said, standing quickly and grabbing another piece of chicken. "Duke, bring my horse."

"Yes, sir, I done did that. It's tied up out front."

Buck kissed his sister and his aunt, then ran out front and climbed onto his horse. He started back toward the road but it was too late. The approaching riders were just coming through the gate at that moment, and from the size of the party, Buck surmised that it was the same patrol Deekus had sighted earlier. They hadn't seen him yet, but it was just a matter of seconds before they did.

Buck tried to turn back, but there was no place to go. There was a high fence on each side of the house, and that kept him from going around. If he cut across the field by the barn, he would be seen.

"Buck!" Becky called. "Here!" Becky was standing by the front door, holding it open for him. "Come through the house!"

Without question, Buck urged his horse up the steps, across the porch, and then through the central hall, the breezeway with which all the southeast Missouri houses were built to aid in cooling during the long, hot summer months. Aunt Ella held the back door open for him and he galloped through, then down the steps and into the swamp behind the house. Thanks to his sister's ingenuity, he managed to get away before the Yankees even knew of his presence.

CHAPTER 3

THE LIGHT, PASSING THROUGH THE DIRTY windowpane, fell upon the face of a medium-size man who, though in his mid-thirties, appeared to be much older. His eyes were dark brown and brooding and his eyebrows and hair were black. There was a long, hook-shaped scar on his cheek, and though most thought it was a war wound it was, instead, the result of an encounter with a rusty nail, suffered three years before the war began.

Col. Sam Armstrong rubbed his finger across the scar on his cheek, a nervous habit of his, as he contemplated the dispatch he had just received from Gen. Sterling Price. He removed the dispatch from its envelope, then held it up to the window so he could read by the light. The originator of the dispatch, General Price, was the overall commander of all Confederate forces in Missouri and Arkansas. He had sent this dispatch, not only to Armstrong, but to every subordinate commander under his jurisdiction, informing them that the war was over. Lee had just surrendered to Grant at a place called Appomattox and General Price was following suit. He was ordering all his subordinate officers to contact the Federal commander nearest their head-quarters to arrange their own surrender.

Armstrong's headquarters was on the banks of the Black River in Clay County, Arkansas. He had chosen this place because it had water and forage for his horses, and because he was far enough re-moved from any regular Yankee Army unit to be safe. Here, too, he had enjoyed the support of the local population, because the sentiments of most of the people in these parts remained pro-South, even after the Federal Army had occupied the state and installed a military governor.

Armstrong sometimes wondered why the peo-ple had remained so loyal. There were no landed gentry here, no large plantations or slaves, nor were there any of the other symbols of the elegant South. These people were, for the most part, small plant-ers with only their sons and daughters to help on the farm. Despite that, their loyalties had remained with the South throughout the entire war.

Though Armstrong publicly praised their loyal-ty, in private, he had little respect for them. To him, one of the biggest mysteries of the war was how the wealthy planters of the South had managed to get so many poor people to fight their battles for them. They had nothing to gain and everything to lose, so why did they do it?

Some might say the same thing about Armstrong. Before the war he had been the overseer on a large plantation in northern Mississippi. He had been paid well for his efforts, and he had a position of authority...but he had never enjoyed the respect of the "good" citizens of the county. In fact, when he once suggested to his employer, Cephus Montgomery, that he would like to call on Cephus's daughter, he was severely rebuked and told to "stay in his place."

When the war started, Armstrong was denied a commission in the regular army because he was "lacking the qualities of a gentleman." He was, however, permitted to raise a company of volunteers to fight as guerrillas. Armstrong did that, and from the first day to this, he had been using his position as a guerrilla chief to feather his nest. While stealing for the South he had actually been putting away quite a bit of money for his own purposes. Every day he had prayed that the war would last a little longer... just long enough to get all the money he needed. Now, according to the dispatch from General Price, the war was over. Col. Sam Armstrong intended to leave this accursed country forever. He was going down to Texas where a man's past or breeding wasn't questioned, and where all that counted was power, and the ability to use it.

There was a knock on the door of the cabin and Armstrong looked up from the dispatch he was holding. The sergeant major stuck his head in.

"Colonel, Cap'n Chaney is back, sir," the sergeant major said.

"Good, good. Send him in," Armstrong said.

"What about the dispatch from General Price?"

"What about it, Sergeant Major?"

"Do you want me to send in the clerk so that you can make a reply?"

Armstrong folded the dispatch and put it in his tunic pocket. The dispatch had come in a sealed envelope, so no one but he knew its contents.

"Uh, no," Armstrong said, thinking for the moment not to disclose the fact that the war was over. He may be able to use this secret information to his own advantage. "It's nothing, the general was just reporting some movement of Yankee troops, that's all. Tell Chaney to report to me at once."

"Yes, sir."

Buck came in the door a moment later. The formalities of saluting had been dropped long before, so Buck just settled into a chair and, without being asked, poured himself a drink of whiskey from the colonel's bottle.

"Did you bring the gold with you?" Armstrong

asked. This was the big chance he had been waiting for and he didn't intend to let it get away from him, just because the war was over.

Buck looked at Armstrong. There was no love lost between these two men. Armstrong was resentful of the fact that Buck had been granted a commission in the regular army, while Buck considered most of Armstrong's war effort as little more than hooliganism.

"No," Buck finally said. He drank the whiskey and felt it bum its way down his throat. He had ridden all night to get here, taking a circuitous route, just in case the Yankees followed him. When he returned, he learned that his friend, Deekus, was dead. "What happened to Deekus?" he asked.

"Ah, yes, it's quite a shame about Sergeant Deekus," Armstrong said. "I'm sorry to report that he was killed in the ambush."

"Whose fault was it?"

"Fault? What do you mean?"

"Deekus was much too good a man to get himself killed in a simple ambush, unless someone made a big mistake."

"There was no big mistake," Armstrong said. "It was just a lucky shot from some Yankee soldier. A stray bullet, that's all."

"Damn!" Buck said. He poured himself another drink. "To come this far and then..." he didn't finish the statement. Instead, he tossed down another drink, then wiped the back of his hand across his mouth.

"Congratulations on your mission," Armstrong said. "You've done a great thing for the South, and I'm certain that General Price will be pleased."

Buck looked at Armstrong for a long moment. "Yeah? Well, I tell you now, Colonel, I'd trade every damned ounce of that gold for Deekus, if I could."

"Where is the gold?" Armstrong asked. "Did you bring it with you?"

"No. I had to hide it."

"Where?"

"Someplace where it's safe."

Armstrong pulled out the dispatch from General Price, but he didn't open it.

"Captain, you've done a fine job so far, but your job isn't completed. I have a dispatch here from General Price. He needs the gold as quickly as we can get it to him. My suggestion to you is that you go back to where you hid it, get it, then bring it back to me." Buck shook his head. "I can't go back," he said. "Not right now. The Yankees will be looking for me."

"They are looking for all of us," Armstrong said impatiently.

"Yeah, but they're looking for me in particular. They may have seen me there."

"Where?"

"At my family's farm."

"Of course, you did live around here, didn't you? Is that where you hid the gold?"

"Yes. I hid it under a loose floorboard in the barn." Armstrong stood up and walked over to the window of the little cabin. He forced himself to remain calm, though the excitement of knowing where the $900,000 was hidden was almost more than he could contain. Outside, smoke from a dozen campfires curled up as the men, unaware that the war was now over, prepared to cook their noon meals. Armstrong turned away from the window and ran his finger across his mustache as he looked at Buck.

"I'll tell you what," he said. "Suppose you report to General Price over in Gainesville. Tell him we have liberated the gold, then ask him for further instructions. It may be that he will want the gold right where it is for a while. I'm certain it is safe there. And if the South can't make use of it right away, then neither can the North."

Buck stood up.

"All right, that suits me," Buck agreed. "I don't mind telling you that I'll be glad to be done with this business, once and for all. I'm a soldier, not a highwayman."

"Yes. Aren't we all?" Armstrong agreed.

Buck rode into General Price's camp after dark that same day. He had spent a lot of time in the saddle over the last three days and he was tired. That, and perhaps the fact that it was dark, explained why he didn't realize that the sentries on guard were Yankees. He was even with them before he noticed. Unfortunately for him, the guards were more alert, and they had him covered as soon as he came into range.

"Get down off that horse, mister," one of them called.

"And do it real slow," the other added.

Slowly, cautiously, Buck swung his leg over, then dismounted. He had his hands up in the air.

"When did you take Gainesville?" he asked.

"Ha!" One of the guards laughed. "What do you mean, Gainesville? We got the whole damned South, friend. The war is over now and we whipped your Rebel asses good."

"The war's over?" Buck asked, surprised by the guard's announcement.

"Yeah. Our general is in there right now, having a sit-down dinner with your general, just like they was old pals or somethin'. Go on up there and have a look-see if you don't believe me."

"May I lower my hands?"

"Yeah, sure," the guard said. "Oh, but we got to take your pistol. We're supposed to disarm all the Rebels we see."

"'Ceptin' the officers. The officers gets to keep their sidearms," the other guard said. "You an officer, mister?"

"Yes," Buck answered. "I'm a captain."

"Can't tell by what you got on. You could be lyin'."

"That's all right. Take my pistol," Buck said. "I just want to see General Price."

"Just drop it on the ground there, then go on up to that buildin'. You'll find him in there with our general, just like we said."

"Thanks."

Buck dropped his pistol, then walked quickly to the building which had been General Price's headquarters. There were two more guards standing outside the door and they, too, were Union soldiers.

"I'm Captain Chaney," Buck said. "I want to speak with General Price."

One of the guards made a motion with his head, and Buck opened the door, then stepped inside.

It was dark in the hallway, but a large square of light was projected into the hall from an open doorway at the far end. A sudden burst of laughter exploded from the room at the end of the hall as several deep voices laughed at someone's remark. Buck moved through the dark toward the light. When he got there, he saw a dinner table laid with elegant china, crystal, and silver. A dozen men were sitting around the table dressed in their finest uniforms, Union and Confederate alike. They were laughing and telling stories and jokes and it could have been the most fashionable house in the country. Instead, it was a meeting of men who, but twenty-four hours before, had been mortal enemies.

It seemed unreal to Buck. Four long years of war, hundreds of thousands of men killed, many more wounded, and now the architects of that war were discussing its outcome as casually as they might discuss the results of a sporting contest. General Price, though the loser, was the gracious host of the dinner, and he was seated at the head of the table. Price's uniform was glittering gray and gold, as bright and shining as the uniforms had been at the many military balls that were held during the early heady days of the war.

"General Price, I must speak with you," Buck called out.

Buck's words brought all conversation to a halt. He was dressed in homespun and it was dirty. He needed a bath and a shave, and his intrusion upon such an elegant affair caused several to gasp in concern. Who was he? Was he an assassin, come to kill one of the generals?

A Yankee lieutenant who was seated at the end of the table nearest the door, turned to look at Buck.

"Who are you, mister?" the Yankee lieutenant demanded.

"I am Captain Buck Chaney, Confederate Cavalry," Buck answered.

"It's all right, Lieutenant Carter, this is one of my officers," General Price said. He smiled at Buck. "Captain Chaney, I see Armstrong got my dispatch. Has he arranged his surrender?"

Buck shook his head in confusion. "What dispatch is that, General?"

"The one I sent yesterday," General Price answered. "General Lee has surrendered his army and the Confederate Government has capitulated. The war is over, and I sent a dispatch to all my subordinate officers in the field yesterday, informing them of that fact."

"Including Colonel Armstrong?"

"Including Colonel Armstrong."

"Colonel Armstrong didn't say anything about it," Buck said.

"That's very odd. I knew he received the dispatch, because my courier has already returned."

"Governor," one of the Union officers said, referring to General Price by that title because, before the war, Price had been governor of Missouri. "You don't suppose this Colonel Armstrong will attempt to carry on the fight on his own, do you?"

"I don't know," General Price admitted. "He is a rather strange and brooding man."

"Where's the gold, Buck?"

Buck looked toward the new voice and saw his brother standing in the door on the other side of the room. Seeing the two men together, one could easily see that they were brothers. Both had blond hair, both had gunmetal gray eyes. The difference between them was one of size. Lance was four inches taller, forty pounds heavier, and broader through the shoulders than Buck. He had been known as the strong one...Buck was known as the quick one, though both were strong and both were quick.

"Lance! What are you doing here?" Buck asked, surprised to see his brother.

General Price chuckled.

"We have all been amused by your daring raid against your brother's transport detail," General Price said. "And by the unique way you...uh...detained them."

"You should have seen them when they came marching into Sikeston, Sterling," General Wilson, the Union general said, laughin'. "Not enough whole cloth among the lot of them to make one decent suit. They were covered with mud from head to toe, and mad as wet hens."

Despite the situation, Buck couldn't help but smile at the verbal picture the Yankee general had painted. He wished he could have seen his brother then.

"Your brother came here to get the gold from me," General Price went on. "He thought you might have brought it to me by now."

"Where is it?" Lance asked. It was clear to Buck that Lance still wasn't amused by the situation.

Buck looked at General Price.

"It's all right, Captain," General Price said. "The war is over. I'm perfectly willing to let the state of Missouri make whatever disposition of the gold it wishes."

"I don't have the gold," Buck said.

"Then what the hell did you do with it?" Lance thundered, angrily.

"Easy, Major," General Wilson said. He looked at Buck. "Captain, I have discussed this matter with General Price, and he has convinced me to accept your taking of the gold as a military operation, rather than a robbery."

"It was a military operation," Buck said quickly.

"And so we are prepared to accept," General Wilson went on. "But, if we are to continue to consider it as such, you must return the shipment to the proper authorities."

"I told you," Buck said. "I don't have the gold."

"Then where is it?" Lance asked again.

Buck looked at General Price. "General, did you send a dispatch to Colonel Armstrong, telling him you needed the gold right away?"

"I sent no such dispatch," General Price said. Buck sighed. "I thought as much."

"Buck, what is it?" Lance asked. "What are you trying to say?"

"I believe Colonel Armstrong has the gold," Buck said.

"You mean you gave it to him?" General Wilson asked.

"No," Buck said. "But I did tell him where to find it."

General Wilson twisted back around and looked at General Price. "You tell me, Sterling. You know this Armstrong person better than I do. Will he surrender to us willingly?"

"Gentlemen, my thought is that, by now, Armstrong is as far away from here as he can get."

"General Wilson," Lance said. "Can you accept the resignation of my commission, right here, right now?" General Wilson looked at Lance. He knew Lance as a courageous soldier who had fought well in every campaign. Lance's first sergeant had explained the circumstances of the loss of the gold shipment so that even that couldn't be held against him. General Wilson knew that if Lance wanted an immediate discharge, there had to be a valid reason.

"I suppose I could," he said. "But what's the big hurry?"

"I'm going after Armstrong," Lance said, removing his jacket and taking the insignia off his hat. "I'm going to find him and bring that gold back."

General Wilson chuckled.

"You don't have to worry about that anymore, Major Chaney. You are no longer responsible. Armstrong will probably be caught someday...and if he isn't, well, such is the fate of war."

"I'm sorry, General, but as far as I'm concerned, I am responsible."

"Well, even if you consider yourself responsible, how do you propose to go about finding him? You don't even know Armstrong, do you?"

"No," Lance said. He looked at his brother. "But Buck knows him."

Buck held up his hands. "I've had enough soldiering," he said. "I'm going back to our farm."

"That's a good idea," General Wilson said. "I think you should do the same thing," he suggested to Lance. "Go back to your farm. Forget about the gold and Armstrong."

"I'm going to find Armstrong," Lance insisted. "And my brother is going to help me. General, my brother was a guerrilla, so that makes him a wanted man. I want you to arrest him."

"What?" Buck said. "Now, hold on here."

"Major Chaney, I'm sure we could work something out," General Wilson said. "As I understand it, your brother spent most of his time in a regular unit."

"I suppose he did," Lance said. "But he was with the guerrillas at the end of the war and that makes him a wanted man. I want him arrested."

"Are you sure about that?" General Wilson asked.

"I'm sure," Lance said, coldly.

"Lance, I know you're sore about me leaving you in your long johns," Buck said. "But aren't you taking this a little too far?"

"I want him arrested and paroled to me," Lance continued. He smiled, pointedly, at his brother. "That way, you'll either ride with me, Buck, or I'll personally see to it that you serve every day of your sentence."

"You would really do that?"

"Yes. I would really do that."

"Well, so much for brotherly love," Buck replied.

CHAPTER 4

A ROPE, AS THICK AS A MAN'S WRIST, RAN from the bow of the Delta Mist to a large rock on the bank of the Ohio River at Cairo, Illinois. The rope was tied to the rock, thus holding the boat in place against the strong pull of the river current. A gangplank stretched from die bow of the boat to the cobblestone bank, providing a way for soldiers and equipment to be loaded aboard.

The riverfront, indeed, the entire city of Cairo, was a beehive of activity, and had been, ever since the war ended. Thousands of soldiers were being brought through Cairo for shipment back home. The great Army of the Republic, now no longer needed, was camped along the riverfront, while its ranks were daily depleted by the debarking river-boats which either headed up the Mississippi to St. Louis and points west, or up the Ohio to Cincinnati, and points east. Some boats, like the Delta Mist, were even heading downriver to Memphis, where enterprising civilians and ex-soldiers hoped to find economic opportunities in the defeated South.

Despite the fact that the soldiers were enduring the hardships of crowded conditions, there was very little complaining. That was because they knew the war was over and they would soon be going home. Also, Cairo was the gathering point for prostitutes and dispensers of spirits, so the soldiers would have entertainment for as long as their mustering-out money lasted.

A man with dark, brooding eyes and black hair, wearing the uniform of a Yankee colonel, stood by the loading ramp, rubbing the scar on his cheek. He watched impassively as two privates struggled to load his two heavy trunks.

"Beg 'pardon, Colonel," a passing sergeant said. "That seems like a pretty big load for just those two men. Would you like me to assign a working party to you?"

"No, thank you," the colonel answered. "These men have been with me from the beginning. They can handle it quite well."

The sergeant looked at the two men as they walked up the gangplank. The gangplank bowed deeply under the load.

"What've you got in those trunks, sir? They look heavy as lead," the sergeant observed.

The colonel glared at him. "What I have in those trunks is my business, Sergeant."

"Yes, sir," the sergeant answered, chastised by the colonel's retort. "I beg your pardon, sir."

A major approached, carrying some papers in his hand. The sergeant used the opportunity to leave, and he saluted both officers as he hurried on.

"Colonel Hardesty?" the major said. The major smiled. "I got them for you."

The colonel returned the major's smile. "I knew you could do it for me, Phil," he said.

The major held up the papers he was holding. "I have new identity papers for you as well as government passage for you and your two men, back down to Memphis. Though why you want to go back there, is beyond me," he said.

"We're all one country again, Phil."

"I guess you're right. By the way, I sure hope you appreciate the effort this took. I had to personally vouch for you as they had no record of you in their files."

"They had no record of me? How could that be?"

"Oh, I'm not at all surprised," the major said. "The records and file keeping have been an absolute mess for these last several months. Mind, I'm not trying to take anything away from you fellows who were actually engaged in battle, but it's been no picnic for those of us back here, either."

"I'm sure it hasn't, Phil," the colonel said condescendingly, as he rubbed the scar on his cheek. "And I'll be sure and remember you to my friend, General Grant."

"Thanks!" Phil said, smiling broadly.

Sam Armstrong had met the major for the first time last night in the bar of the Little Egypt Hotel in downtown Cairo. He had cultivated the major so that now, they were fast friends. Sam told the major that all his records had been lost in the sinking of the Morganna, a steamboat which, while coming north from Memphis, had exploded and sunk with the loss of hundreds of lives.

The major believed Sam's story and Sam Armstrong, Confederate guerrilla, now had papers which identified him as Col. Sam Hardesty of the Union Army. He had taken the name from an article he read in the local newspaper, the Cairo Pilot. Through the gullibility of the major, Sam also had government tickets to help him escape.

"I appreciate it, Phil. I appreciate it more than you'll ever know," Sam said, reaching out and shaking the major's hand.

"Well, I must get back," the major said. He chuckled. "You know what they are all upset about now? The Rebels are supposed to have stolen a big gold shipment during the last week of the war."

"Do they have any idea where the money is?"

"Not the slightest," the major said. "For a while this morning I was afraid we were going to have to open all the trunks coming aboard any of the boats. Can you imagine what a job that would have been?"

"Would have been?"

"Yeah. Thank God someone finally got a little sense. There have already been twenty boats leave here and none of their stuff was searched. If you ask me, I think the money is buried somewhere."

"Yeah," Sam said, breathing a little easier now that he knew his trunks wouldn't be opened and searched. "I'm sure you're right."

"Good luck, Colonel."

"Thanks, Phil. Thanks for everything," Sam said. Shortly after the major left, Clay and Carl Beekman, Sam's two "privates" came down the gangplank to pick up the remaining trunk. Sam followed them back onto the boat and watched as they put the trunk in the cargo well with the other luggage.

"I still think we should put these in your stateroom," Clay grumbled. "I don't like leaving that much money around just for the—"

"Watch your mouth!" Sam said sharply, interrupting Clay in midsentence. "If you want everyone to know what we have in those trunks, why don't you just paint a sign?"

"Well, I wasn't aimin' to tell anyone," Clay replied. "You couldn't prove that by me," Sam said. "You were talking loud enough that anyone could overhear you. Just keep quiet and everything will be all right. If we take them to my stateroom someone might get suspicious about trunks that I'm so particular about. This way these trunks are no different from any other baggage on this boat."

"The colonel's right, Clay," Carl said to his brother. "Besides, we agreed that if he would let us in on it, he'd be the boss, remember?"

"Yeah, I remember," Clay said. "But we ain't in the army no more and I don't intend to be treated like we are. I mean, seems to me like we're more partners than anything else."

"You're quite right, Clay," Sam said in a more conciliatory tone. "But for the time being we must continue to act as soldiers. Do you understand?"

"Yeah," Clay said. "I understand. But that's only for the time bein'. When we get to where we're goin', I ain't takin' no more orders."

Sam looked at the two Beekman brothers. After he learned from Buck Chaney where the gold was hidden he took the Beekmans along to help him retrieve it. He had to take them because there was no way he could get that much gold out by himself. So far he had them convinced that it would be better to let him handle everything, and they were going along with it. He would keep them with him as long as it served his interest. But if it ever reached the point that he thought them no longer useful, he would find some way to get rid of them.

Buck and Lance stopped at the gate which led onto Doubletree Farm and looked at the sign. A grasshopper was clinging to the faded lettering and a clump of weeds had grown up in front of the sign. Lance dismounted and pulled the weeds so that the sign was clearly visible.

"That sign needs to be redone. It won't be long to where you can't even read it," Lance observed.

"Yeah. Pa must be turning over in his grave," Buck said, as he looked up and down the fencerow. "Look at this place. It is really run-down."

"It's a damned shame," Lance said. "This was the best-kept farm in New Madrid County." He tossed the weed he had just pulled aside, then climbed back onto his horse. The saddle creaked under his weight. "Now I feel guilty every time I see it. There's so much work to be done."

"If you see that, why are you so all-fired ready to go off on a wild-goose chase?"

The two brothers rode through the gate and started up the long road toward the house. Their horses frightened up a rabbit which bounded down the lane in front of them for several feet before darting off into the safety of the tall grass.

"What wild-goose chase?"

"You know what wild-goose chase. I'm talking about going after the gold. Why do you want to do that?"

"In case you have forgotten, I was responsible for that gold," Lance reminded him.

"What difference does that make? Let it be, Lance," Buck said. "Think of the number of men we lost... good men, who died in this war. We were responsible for them, too, but we can't bring them back. Your pride is wounded because you lost the gold. .But is your wounded pride greater than your concern over the lives of the men you lost?"

"No, of course not," Lance answered. "But that's done, and there's nothing I can do about it. I can find the gold."

"Maybe," Buck agreed. "But the war is over. I say let it stay over. Let's you and me get on with our lives. There's work to be done here. Good, honest work, and I think we should stay here and do it. We've given up enough."

Lance stopped his horse and when he stopped, Buck did, too. Lance reached down and patted the neck of his animal.

"Buck, do you really think we can work together again...as brothers?"

"My God, Lance," Buck answered. "If we can't do it, then what the hell chance does the country have of getting back together again? We've got to try. We owe it to ma and pa. We owe it to Becky, and we owe it to ourselves. We've got to try."

Lance smiled, and it was the first genuine smile to pass between the two brothers since they had met in Gainesville.

"All right," he said. "If you're game to stay here and start pulling weeds, I guess I'm willing to let the authorities deal with your Colonel Armstrong."

Buck reached out and took Lance's hand in his own. They shook hands for a moment, then leaned across to embrace each other.

"Mr. Lance! Mr. Buck! Thank the Lord, you all is back!" Duke shouted. Duke came running down the road toward them.

"Look at old Duke run." Buck chuckled. "I haven't seen him run that fast since you threw a rock into that hornets' nest."

"Me! You're the one threw that rock," Lance said, laughing.

"It's a tragedy!" Duke was shouting. "It's the most worst tragedy they ever was!"

As Duke came closer, Lance and Buck realized that there was something drastically wrong.

"What is it?" Lance asked. The smile left his face and his expression reflected his concern. "What's he saying?"

"I don't know," Buck replied. "But I aim to find

out." He slapped his heels against the side of his horse and his horse broke quickly into a gallop. Lance did the same with his horse, and they began to close the distance between them and Duke. When they got closer, Buck could see that Duke was crying! "Duke? Duke, what is it?" Buck asked.

"It's Miss Becky," Duke said. "Oh, Lord, Mr. Buck, Mr. Lance. When your Aunt Ella and me come back from goin' into town yesterday, we found her."

"Found her? What do you mean, you found her?" Buck asked.

"She be dead, Mr. Buck. Somebody done come along and do awful things to that sweet little old girl, and after they do them awful things, why, they killed her."

The murder of Becky Chaney brought the people of New Madrid County together like nothing had in years. Hundreds of mourners came to her funeral. Soldiers in Federal blue and ex-soldiers in the homespun butternut of the Confederacy stood side by side, many showing the scars of war, some with one leg, some with one arm. Just weeks earlier these same men had been bitter enemies...now they were united in their sorrow. Neighbors who had not spoken since before the war wept together as Becky's coffin was lowered into the ground.

Aunt Ella sat in a chair beside the grave, while Lance and Buck stood to either side of her, greeting their friends and neighbors as they filed slowly by. Finally, when the last mourner had climbed into the wagon, and Duke had come for Aunt Ella, only Lance and Buck remained at the grave side. They dismissed the grave digger and, each taking a shovel, began to close the grave themselves.

The dirt made a ringing sound as it left the shovel, then a hollow clumping as it landed on the top of the coffin. Except for the sound of the shoveling, the two men worked in silence for several moments. Then, when the grave was nearly closed, Buck spoke.

"I thought I knew him better than that."

"Who?"

"Col. Sam Armstrong," Buck said.

"What do you mean?"

"I'm going to kill him, Lance. I'm going to kill the son of a bitch."

"Armstrong?" Lance stopped shoveling. "Look here, Buck, is there something you're not telling me? Are you saying Armstrong did this? Armstrong raped and killed Becky?"

"It had to be him," Buck said. "He's the only one who knew where I hid the gold."

"Yes, but what does that have to do with Becky?"

"I hid the gold under the floor of the barn," Buck said. "Becky must have happened onto him when he was taking it out. I guess that's when he...did it.

It's my fault. I never should have told him. It's all my fault."

The two brothers had completely filled the hole by now, and a small mound of dirt was raised over the grave. Lance patted it down smooth with the back of his shovel, but he didn't say anything.

"Didn't you hear me?" Buck asked. "I said it was all my fault! I'm responsible for this!"

Lance still said nothing.

"Well, hit me, damn you!" Buck shouted. "Do something! Say something!"

Lance looked at Buck and there was a great sadness in his eyes. Finally he sighed.

"It's as much my fault as it is yours," Lance said. "I could have come here to the farm the moment we got word the war was over, but I was too proud. I had to go to Gainesville. I had to try and recover the gold. We're a fine pair, brother. We spent four years trying to kill each other, we drove ma and pa to an early grave, and in the end, when our sister needed us, neither one of us was here. Doesn't look to me like either one of us can ever hold our heads up around here anymore."

"You're right about that," Buck agreed. "So what do you suggest we do about it?"

"I suggest we sell the farm...everything but the house...and we give the house to Aunt Ella. We'll get enough from the farm to keep her for the rest of her life."

"And go after Armstrong, right?"

"Right. Are you going with me?"

"You're damn right I'm going with you," Buck replied. "Only, I think there's something you should know."

"What's that?"

"If we find that gold, I don't have any intention of returning it," he said. "I gave up too much during the last four years to just take the money back to the government and say, 'Here, take it with my compliments.' I figure they owe me something."

"We're going to give it back," Lance said.

"No, we're not."

Lance looked at his brother for a long moment, then he sighed. "We do both agree that we want Colonel Armstrong, don't we?"

"Yes," Buck said. "We agree on that."

"Then we'll work together until we find Armstrong. The gold will just have to take care of itself."

"All right, I'll go along with that," Buck agreed. "We work together to find Armstrong...but when it comes to the gold, we're on our own."

CHAPTER 5

Texas, Two Years Later

THE NEARBY MESA ROSE LIKE A HUGE BLACK slab against the velvet texture of the sky. Overhead the stars spread their diamond glitter across the heavens, while far to the east a tiny bar of pearl gray light gave the first indication of impending dawn. The wind, which had moaned and whistled across the rocky crags and sharp precipices all through the long night was quiet now, and a predawn stillness had descended over the land.

Lance Chaney yawned and stretched to work out the kinks of having spent the night on the ground, then ran his hand across his lower jaw to feel a little stubble of beard. He decided he could go a few more days without shaving. He preferred to be clean-shaven but when he was in the open country he often let it go longer than normal.

Lance got a fire going then measured out a careful amount of his precious coffee. A moment later the air was permeated by the rich aroma of the beverage. As we waited for it, he looked over at his horse, securely taked out from the night before.

"All right, horse, you tell me," Lance asked. "You and I sure came up with nothing. Now, how about Buck? Did he find out anything?"

The horse blew and pawed at the ground.

"Yeah," Lance said, grinning. He poured himself a cup of coffee. "That's just about what I thought you'd say. Well, we're supposed to meet him in Sulphur Springs today, and compare notes. I hope he's had better luck than we have."

The coals from his campfire glowed cherry red in the predawn darkness, and Lance threw some more wood on to enjoy its warmth. Though it would be hot when the sun was high, it had been cold and damp on the ground last night, and the fire felt good to him this morning.

"Listen, if he found something, he wouldn't go off without me, would he?" Lance waited for a second, then he answered his own question. "No, he's my brother and brothers don't treat brothers that way." Lance laughed. "Wait a minute, this is Buck we're talking about, isn't it? He damn sure would go off on his own if he thought he could get away from me. The only thing is, he knows that no matter where he goes, I'll be right there."

Suddenly, and for no discernable reason, Lance realized that he wasn't alone. The hackles rose on the back of his neck and he stiffened.

"I reckon you must think I'm about half-nuts, talking out loud like this," Lance said calmly. "Come on in. It'll be a pleasure to have someone other than my horse to talk to."

Lance heard a chuckle. "I figured I couldn't get this close without you'd know I was here. Anyhow, I seet your fire and smelt your coffee and figured you'd be up to sharin' a bit," a voice called from the dark.

Lance chastised himself for not being more alert. He had been so deeply lost in thought a few moments earlier that whoever it was had been able to approach this close without being seen or heard. Such laxity could sometimes prove fatal.

Lance looked over toward his bedroll. His gun belt lay by the saddle which had been his pillow. He had put it there so he could get to it easily in his sleep. He had not yet put on the gun belt, so if the voice in the dark had the drop on him, his best bet would be to do nothing which would arouse the suspicions of his mysterious visitor. He held his arms out so that the man in the dark could see that he was making no attempt to go for a gun.

"Like I said, I'd be pleased to have the company." Lance pointed to the coffeepot which was suspended over the dancing flames of his fire. "There's plenty of coffee here. Come on in and have a cup."

Lance turned to search the darkness for the man, but saw nothing at first. Then he heard the sound of someone walking and finally the man emerged from the darkness into the golden bubble of light put out by the little campfire.

"Where's your horse?" Lance asked.

"Oh, I left him back a-ways," the man answered. "Found some sweet grass for him."

The man who came into the campsite was a tall, thin man. He had slick black hair, dark brown eyes, and high cheekbones over sunken cheeks. He was wearing a long black coat and a thin, black string tie. Even his hat was black, and he touched the brim of it in greeting. He was carrying a Navy Colt in a well- used holster. Lance saw the man's eyes take him in, then dart, ever-so-quickly, to Lance's bed-roll where he saw Lance's hardware. The stranger smiled, though the smile was so small as to nearly be imperceptible.

Lance handed him a cup.

"I thank you kindly," the man said. He filled his cup with coffee, then squatted down on his heels to take a drink, slurping it through his extended lips to cool it. "Prospectin'?"

"No," Lance said. "Just traveling through."

"Ain't much for the traveler in these parts," the man suggested.

"I'm going to meet my brother in Sulphur Springs. I figure I'll be there by nightfall."

The stranger nodded, then finished his coffee and stood up. He looked toward Lance's bedroll.

"You got a poke?"

"Mister, I don't consider that any of your business," Lance replied calmly.

The man sucked air through his teeth, then slowly, but deliberately, pulled his pistol.

"Well, sir, now I reckon I'm goin' to have to make it my business," he said. "You see, I've been prospectin' in these parts so long that I've run out of my own poke. Truth to tell, I don't even have a horse no more. So what I'm aimin' to do is just shoot you and take what you got; your food, your bedroll, your saddle, and your horse. I reckon that'll keep me goin' a little while longer."

"You aren't showing much gratitude for my hospitality," Lance complained.

The stranger chuckled. "No, sir, I guess I'm not at that. But, you see, that's the price you pay for not wearin' a gun in these parts."

"Oh, that," Lance said, dismissing his pistol with a shrug of his shoulders. "Well, it's my brother who is good with a gun. I've always had to get by on my strength and wits."

The stranger laughed out loud. "Strength and wits, is it?" he said. "Well, I'm afraid that's not good enough. You could be as strong as Samson and as smart as Solomon and you won't be able to get yourself out of this mess."

"You know your Bible," Lance said.

"I read it from time to time to while away the lonely hours," the stranger admitted.

"Too bad none of it has ever taken hold."

"Well, that's just the way of it, sometimes. But I tell you what, I'll give you time to make your peace."

"Thanks," Lance said.

Lance bowed his head as if he were about to say a prayer. Suddenly he made a feint toward his pistol, then surprised his assailant by jumping the other way. The dark stranger had anticipated Lance's moving toward his gun, so he squeezed off a shot in that direction. The gun flashed bright orange in the dim morning and even though he missed, Lance could feel the air of the bullet as it whizzed by. Lance went down on the ground, then rolled away from his bedroll just as the stranger fired a second time. This time the bullet was so close that it kicked dirt into Lance's face.

As Lance rolled on the ground avoiding even a third shot, he reached the edge of the fire and picked up a burning brand, then tossed it at the gunman. The gunman threw up his hands to avoid it and, when he did, Lance rushed at him, charging him like a maddened bull.

The gunman, in trying to avoid Lance's charge, dropped his pistol, and had a moment's indecision as to whether he should try and recover it, or get away. That moment of indecision cost him, for Lance wrapped both arms around him and began squeezing. He squeezed until he felt bones breaking in the would-be assailant's body. Splintered rib bones pierced the man's lungs, then penetrated his heart. He made a choking, rattling sound, then he was quiet. Lance let him go and he fell to the ground as limp as an empty shirt. When Lance looked down at him, he saw a small trickle of blood coming from his lips.

Lance backed away slowly, dusting himself off as he did so.

"A little jerky, some coffee, and a horse," Lance said under his breath. "That's all I had. Mister, you paid a hell of a price for a chance at such a little reward."

Forty miles north, and ten hours later on that same day, Buck Chaney slapped a silver coin on the bar in Sulphur Springs' only saloon, and the barkeep came down to serve him. The barkeep had noticed how Buck was armed. He was wearing a single Navy Colt, hanging low in a quick-draw holster on the right side of a bullet-studded belt.

The barkeep served Buck the best whiskey the saloon had to offer, for he had learned long ago to recognize the difference between men who were bluster and show, and men who were business. Buck was obviously a man who was all business.

Buck thanked the barkeep with a slight nod, then slowly surveyed the interior of the saloon. It was typical of the many he had seen over the last two years. A piano ground away at the back of the place, a dozen or more men filled the room, and tobacco smoke hovered under the ceiling like a cloud. It was twilight now, and as daylight disappeared, flickering coal oil lanterns combined with the smoke to make the room seem even hazier.

During the past two years these kinds of surroundings had, somehow, become Buck's heritage. He had been redefined by saloons, cow towns, stables, dusty streets, and open prairies, all of which he encountered on his never-ending search.

"Armstrong, you are out there, somewhere," Buck said under his breath, every morning of his life. "You are out there, somewhere, and I'm going to find you."

Buck wasn't making the search alone. His brother, Lance, was searching with him. Sometimes they searched together, sometimes, in order to cover more territory, their trails separated. But always they came back together, and always they kept the same goal in mind. They were going to find Armstrong and the missing gold. They had different ideas as to what to do with the gold if they found it. As to Armstrong, however, both brothers were in agreement.

This time Buck had something. He was convinced that after two long years of false trails and bad information, he finally had an idea of where Armstrong was. Lance was supposed to meet him here, in Sulphur Springs, sometime this evening. The question that was plaguing Buck was: Should he tell him? "Hey, you! Is your name Chaney?"

The man who interrupted Buck's reverie was a tall man with a bushy red beard.

"Yes," Buck said.

"Which one would it be? Buck or Lance?"

"I'm Buck Chaney."

The bearded man smiled, showing tobacco-stained teeth, then he turned to face Buck. That was when Buck saw that he was already holding a gun in his hand, and he was pointing it at Buck.

"Well, now, Buck Chaney. You're just the man I been lookin' for."

"You've been lookin' for me? Why?"

"There's a fellow I know got a little reward out for you," the bearded man said. "You and your brother. From what I hear, he's offered five hundred dollars to anyone who will kill you."

Buck smiled. "Five hundred dollars, you say? And to think that people used to tell me I'd never amount to anything."

"You're pretty cheerful for a man that's about to die," Redbeard said.

"Oh, I'm not about to die," Buck said easily. He picked up his drink with his left hand, then turned to face the man. "You are."

"Me?" Redbeard laughed and looked at the others in the saloon, all of whom had interrupted their own conversations to listen in on this life-and-death drama that was suddenly being played out before them. "Did you all hear that? This here fellow says I'm the one goin' to die, when I'm the one holdin' the gun on him."

The others began to move away then, positioning themselves far enough back to be out of any line of fire, yet close enough so as not to miss anything that might happen.

It grew quiet in the saloon, so quiet that the large grandfather's clock against the wall ticked loudly. In one of the rooms upstairs, squeaking bedsprings and the forced moans of pleasure from a Soiled Dove could be heard, but such was the drama of the moment that no one appeared to notice.

"Now, just how are you goin' to kill me, Mr. Chaney, with me holdin' the gun on you?" Redbeard asked.

"Simple," Buck answered. He put the drink down on the bar. "When you see me reach for my gun, you pull the trigger."

Redbeard laughed. "Oh, don't you worry none about that," he said. "I'll pull the trigger all right."

Buck relaxed. Without knowing the explanation of why, he had already learned that the slowest part of any draw was the time it took to think about it. He could draw and shoot his pistol in one action. If Redbeard actually did wait until Buck started his draw before he pulled the trigger, Redbeard would still be thinking about pulling the trigger while Buck was already doing it. It was almost an unfair edge...but Buck didn't challenge this man...this man challenged Buck.

Suddenly Buck had the pistol in his hand, moving so quickly that he had it out and shooting before practically anyone, including Redbeard, was aware that he was even making his move. In fact, Buck had such an advantage that he was able to afford the luxury of not having to kill Redbeard. Instead he aimed for the shoulder and hit Redbeard high...too high for the bullet to hit any vital organs, but solidly enough to make him drop his gun with a howl of pain. He reached up to grab the wound, then looked at Buck with eyes which were wide in amazement.

"How...how the hell did you do that?" he asked.

"Huh-uh," Buck replied, smiling at him. "I can't give away all my secrets. Now, kick the gun over here."

Redbeard did as he was instructed, and the gun slid across the floor to Buck. Buck picked it up, then emptied the loads, and handed the pistol to the barkeep.

"You keep it for him," he said. "He's liable to get hurt playing with it."

The others in the saloon laughed loudly then, and Redbeard, still holding his hand over his shoulder wound, left the saloon in disgrace.

"Barkeep," Buck said.

"Yes, Mr. Chaney?"

"How many trains go west from here?"

"Two," the barkeep said proudly. "One in the morning, one in the afternoon."

Buck slid some money across the bar. "Get me two tickets on tomorrow morning's westbound train," he said.

"Two tickets, sir?"

"Yes. And when my brother asks for me, give them to him and tell him to wake me up in time so that I don't miss the train."

"Yes, sir," the barkeep said. "Two tickets on the morning westbound, give them to your brother, tell him to wake you in time that you don't miss the train. I'll take care of it, Mr. Chaney. You can count on me."

CHAPTER 6

BUCK SAT LOOKING OUT THE WINDOW OF
the train as the terrain rolled by. He was on his way
to Brenham, Texas, and his brother was in the seat
beside him, with his knees jammed up against the
seat in front, his arms folded across his chest, and
his hat down over his eyes. Lance was snoring softly.

The trip from Sulphur Springs had been long and
tiring with nothing outside to break up the scenery except gently rolling mesquite land. The view
inside hadn't been particularly attractive either,
consisting mostly of immigrant families, washed-
out, poor, and eager looking, and overweight
drummers. A while back a young cowboy who was
wearing an ivory- handled pistol, leather chaps, and
highly polished silver rowels got on the train. He
had swaggered back and forth through the car a few
times, but Buck paid little attention to him.

By the time they reached Hempstead the outside scenery, because of the Brazos River, improved a little. It improved inside as well, when a very pretty young woman boarded the train. As she boarded, she had smiled, prettily, shyly, at Buck, and he smiled back.

The young cowboy in the chaps and silver rowels evidently knew her, and he called her by name—Lucinda—and he moved to sit near her. Buck put her out of his mind and began to think of what lay ahead. He was sure, this time, that they had located Armstrong. The break he had been looking for came, oddly enough, in a newspaper article. He reached into his pocket and pulled it out, unfolded it, and read it again.

Railroad Built from Brenham to Barlow

The enterprising town of Barlow, Texas, some seventeen miles west of Brenham, has recently been joined to Brenham by a new railroad, built by Colonel S. Barlow.

Colonel S. Barlow, the leading citizen of Barlow and a Confederate hero of the Battle of Gettysburg in the late war, has been of particular value to the prosperity and growth of that part of Texas. After the war, Colonel Barlow settled there where he commenced to rebuild an abandoned town. In addition to the Barlow Railroad, he owns the town's newspaper and most of its businesses. He is also the largest rancher in the area, owning Gold

DustRanchwhichconsistsofoveronehundredthousandacresof rangeland.ColonelBarlowplanstoshipoverfifteenthousand headofcattlethisyear.ThecitizensofthetownoweColonelBar-lowavoteofthanks,forwiththeadditionoftherailroad,Barlow is guaranteed to grow and prosper.

The thing which most interested Buck was the name of Colonel Barlow's ranch. He was calling it the Gold Dust Ranch. And since the $900,000 was in gold dust, that seemed a connection.

Of course, nothing else fit. Buck didn't really expect Armstrong to keep his name, so he wasn't looking for someone named Armstrong. Also, this colonel supposedly fought in the Battle of Gettysburg. Armstrong certainly didn't fit that description either. Still, if he could lie about his name, he could just as easily lie about his background. He was a wealthy man who had come to the territory immediately after the war, and he did name his ranch the Gold Dust. Buck thought that was too much of a coincidence to pass up, and Lance agreed with him.

There was another thing to consider. Yesterday, someone tried to shoot him for a five-hundred-dollar reward. Buck knew there was no paper out on him from any legitimate law enforcement agency. By now he had even been granted amnesty for having once been a guerrilla. Therefore, if someone had offered a reward of five hundred dollars for him and his brother, that someone had to be Col. Sam Armstrong. The fact that someone tried to collect on it yesterday, meant that they were close. Very close.

"Brenham! We're comin' into Brenham, folks," the conductor said, walking quickly through the car. He stopped beside Buck and Lance. "You said you wanted to saddle your horses before we arrived?"

"Uh, yeah," Buck answered. "How far are we?"

"Just under two miles, sir," the conductor answered.

Buck poked his brother, who grunted, then sat up and ran his hand through his hair.

"What is it?" he growled.

"Brenham," Buck said. "The conductor says we can go up and saddle our horses now."

"You go ahead. I want to get a drink of water," Lance said.

Buck got up and walked forward, toward the stock car, while Lance walked back to the water scuttle. When Buck stepped out onto the vestibule, he saw the girl and the silver-bedecked cowboy standing on the platform between cars.

"Please," the girl was saying. "Please, just leave me alone."

"Come on, I seen the way you was lookin' at me

at the Cattlemen's Ball last week. You ain't foolin' no one by playin' hard to get."

Buck had already put his hand on the door to go into the next car when he heard the exchange, and he stopped and looked back at them. He was reluctant to interfere in any discussion between a man and woman because he knew that playing reluctant was often part of a woman's courting ritual. In this case, however, the expression on the young lady's face and the tone of her voice told him that she wasn't playing a game. She was serious when she told the man she didn't want to be bothered.

"Mister, why don't you go on back in the car and leave the lady alone?" Buck asked.

The cowboy looked toward Buck as if shocked that anyone would butt in.

"What did you say to me?"

"I told you to go on back into the car and leave the lady alone."

"Why don't you just go to hell?" the cowboy growled menacingly. He turned back to the girl as if dismissing Buck, but Buck wouldn't be dismissed. He stepped back across the gap between the two cars then grabbed the cowboy by the scruff of the neck and the seat of his pants.

"Hey, what the—" the cowboy shouted, but whatever the fourth word was going to be was lost in the rattle of cars and his own surprised scream as Buck threw him, bodily, from the train. The cowboy hit on the down slope of the track base, then bounced and rolled through the rocks and scrub weed alongside the train. Buck leaned out far enough to see him stand and shake his fist, but by then the train had swept on away from him.

"He'll be all right," Buck said. "He'll have a little walk into town, is all."

The girl laughed, and even above the sound of the train, Buck could hear the musical lilt to her laugh. Lance came out onto the platform at that moment.

"What is it?" Lance asked. "What happened?"

"The fellow with all the silver just got off the train," Buck said easily. He looked at the girl. "I hope I wasn't out of line, miss. I hope you were serious when you told him you wanted him to leave you alone. I mean, you did seem to know him. At least, I heard him call you by name. It is Lucinda, isn't it?"

"Yes. Lucinda Gray. My father ranches near Barlow, that's why I know him. His name is Jack Wiggins and he works for Colonel Barlow. I know him, but believe me, he is no friend of mine. I'm afraid he'll be no friend of yours, either. I hope you haven't made a dangerous enemy. Especially since he works for Colonel Barlow."

"Colonel Barlow? That would be the man who owns the Gold Dust Ranch?" Lance asked.

"Yes," the girl said. "Colonel Samuel Barlow, the

self-styled, King of the Range."

"From all I've heard, the Colonel has been a big benefactor to the area," Lance said.

"If you call running all the small ranchers off by diverting the water a benefit, then I suppose you could call him a benefactor," Lucinda said. Her tone was as harsh as her words.

"Then I take it you don't like Colonel Barlow?"

Lucinda's expression changed slightly, becoming more guarded. "Are you two coming to work for the Colonel?" she asked, anxiously.

"Not necessarily," Buck said.

"Although we are looking for work," Lance added.

"I hope you don't work for the Colonel," Lucinda said. "Although, of course, I have no right to tell you who you should, or shouldn't work for."

The train started slowing then, and Lucinda leaned out to look forward. "I have to get off here," she said. "This is where I catch the train to Barlow."

Lucinda excused herself again, then walked back into the car.

"Now that's one pretty woman," Buck observed.

"That she is," Lance agreed. "But she certainly doesn't like the gentleman we have come to see."

"Did you hear her? His name is Sam," Buck said. "I know he's the one, Lance, I can feel it. Do you suppose he has any of the gold left?"

"I don't know," Lance answered. "But I'm not worried about that right now. If Barlow is Armstrong then I want him. First things first."

Lance and Buck tied their horses to a hitching rail in front of the Red Lion Saloon a few minutes later, then walked up to the bar for a couple of beers to wash away the soot and ash of the long train ride. The man behind the bar drew two mugs and set them, with foaming heads, in front of the brothers. Buck slid a ten-cent piece of silver across the counter, then he drank the first one down without taking away the mug. He wiped the foam away from his lips and slid the empty mug toward the barkeep.

"That one was for thirst," he said. "This one is for taste."

With the second beer in his hand, Buck turned his back to the bar and looked out over the saloon. There were half-a-dozen tables scattered about. A card game was in progress at one of them, while the other tables held only drinkers and conversationalists. A bar-girl sidled up to the two brothers. She was heavily painted and showed the dissipation of her profession. There was no humor or life left in her eyes, and when she saw that neither Buck nor Lance expressed an interest in her, she turned and walked back to sit by the piano player.

The piano player wore a small, round derby hat, and kept his sleeves up with garter belts. He was pounding away on the keyboard, but the music was practically lost amidst the noise of two dozen, separate conversations.

Buck was on his third beer when the batwing doors swung open and Jack Wiggins came in. He had scratches and bruises on his face, and his clothes were dirty and torn.

"Jack? What the hell happened to you?" someone asked.

"Some son of a bitch pushed me off the train," Jack said.

Everyone in the saloon laughed.

"Goddamnit! It isn't funny!" Jack said. "I was just standin' there on the vestibule, mindin' my own business, when he sneaked up behind me and shoved me off. I never even saw him."

"You weren't minding your own business," Buck said easily, taking another swallow of his beer. He pulled the mug back down and wiped the back of his hand across his mouth before he continued. "You were making unwanted advances toward a young woman."

Buck's voice cut above the laughter and the buzz of the saloon, and at his challenging words, everything suddenly grew very quiet. Jack looked toward the bar and saw Buck.

"You!" he shouted in an angry voice, pointing at Buck. "You're the one who did this to me!"

"How do you know he's the one, Jack, if you never even seen him?" someone asked, and everyone in the saloon laughed.

"Pull your gun, you bastard!" Jack yelled at Buck. "Pull your gun! I'm goin' to shoot your eyes out!" The laughter stopped then, and there was a quick scrape of chairs and tables as everyone scrambled to get out of the way. Only Lance didn't move away from Buck. Lance looked over at the barkeep, who had ducked down behind the bar.

"Oh, there you are," Lance said easily. "Could I have another beer?"

"Mister, are you crazy?" the barkeep hissed. "Get out of the line of fire!"

Lance chuckled, then looked back toward Jack Wiggins, who was standing in the doorway with his arm crooked, just above his pistol.

"Oh, you mean him?" he asked, calmly. "Ah, don't worry about him. As soon as he twitches, Buck will put him down. He won't even get off a shot. Listen," he continued, as if Jack Wiggins were no longer even in his thoughts. "Don't put as big a head on it this time. The last one was mostly foam."

Several people gasped at Lance's easy words and calm manner.

"Could I have that beer?" he asked.

The barkeep raised up just far enough to take Lance's mug, then he drew another beer and handed it to him.

"Thanks," Lance said. He blew the foam off, then turned around. He was standing right next to Buck, clearly in the line of fire of a gunfight should break out. He took a swallow of his beer and stared at Jack over the rim of the glass.

Jack, like the others, had heard Lance's calm declaration and was now observing his disdain. Jack's hand began to shake.

"Mister," Lance said, "if I were you, I'd leave now. You've got the shakes so bad that my brother's liable to make a mistake. He's liable to think you're going for your gun, when all you're really doing is peeing in your pants."

Jack opened and closed his fingers several times, then, quickly, he turned and hurried back through the doors. His retreat was greeted with the laughter of everyone in the saloon.

"Step up to the bar, boys," someone shouted joyfully. "The drinks are on the house. Anytime I can see one of Colonel Barlow's boys backed down like that, it's worth a round."

"Beer!"

"Whiskey!"

More than a score of voices called out their orders as everyone rushed to the bar. The man who was buying the drinks came down to stand beside Buck and Lance.

"You fellows are new around here, aren't you?"

he asked.

"You might say that," Buck answered.

"I thought so. Most people would have buckled under to Wiggins."

"Is he really that fast?" Lance asked.

"Who knows? He's fast enough, I suppose," the man replied. "But that's not the point. The point is, he's one of the Colonel's men, and the Colonel has got a regular army. You cross one of them and you cross them all."

"I take it you aren't a friend of the Colonel," Buck observed.

The man laughed. "You've got that right," he said. He stuck out his hand. "The name is Langdon, Jess Langdon. I own a spread over near Barlow. I'm one of the few ranchers left who can make that claim. Colonel Barlow has run most of the others off."

"You would be a neighbor of Gray's?" Buck asked. Langdon smiled. "Indeed I am, sir, indeed I am. No finer man ever lived than Emerson Gray. Do you know him?"

"No," Buck admitted. "But I did meet his daughter on the train. She was the young woman the cowboy was bothering."

"Then I am doubly in your debt, sir," Langdon said. "Not only for putting one of Barlow's men to shame, but for defending the honor of the fairest young lady on the range. If there is ever anything I can do for you, please let me know."

"Tell us more about Colonel Barlow," Lance asked. "Where does he come from?"

"He claims to have come from Virginia," Langdon said.

"Claims?"

"We aren't too particular about a man's past out here," Langdon went on. "Since the war and all, we figure every man's got a right to start a new life. We generally let a fellow make whatever claim he wants, we see no need to question it, less there is a particular reason."

"Has Barlow given you a reason?"

"Not exactly," Langdon admitted. "He has been a most disagreeable neighbor, but everything he has done has been legal."

"How did one man come to control so much, so quickly?" Lance asked.

"I guess he's just a shrewd businessman. From all I've heard, he's built up his empire on borrowed money and guts. He's never paid cash for anything."

"Are you sure?" Buck asked in surprise. "What about gold dust?"

"His ranch?"

"No. I mean real gold dust. Might he have made some of his deals using gold dust?"

Langdon laughed. "No," he answered. "There is a story about how he came to name his ranch that. It seems he went into the bank to borrow the money and the banker asked him why he wanted so much land. The banker told him there was nothing out there but dust. Colonel Barlow allowed as that may be so, but by the time he got finished with it, it would be gold dust. And, much as I hate to admit it, he's nearly made good on his promise."

"And the banker loaned him the money?"

"Every penny of it," Langdon said. "Like I say, I got no likin' for Colonel Barlow, but give the Devil his due. He's built himself an empire on sheer guts and gall."

"What about this town, Barlow?"

"It used to be called Long Point. Folks built it because they thought the Houston and Central Texas Railroad would come that far. But when the war started the railroad stopped building, so people just abandoned the town. Barlow bought it up for a song and he got to ownin' so much of the town that he renamed it for himself, and nobody argued with him. Now, with the railroad, it's a boomin' little town, complete with a bank, a feed store, a general store, a couple of saloons, and a hotel."

"Does Barlow own all of it?" Buck asked.

"No, sir. There's a few good people still hanging on to things in the town," Langdon said. "And I own the hotel and saloon myself. That is, I own it with a partner."

"Who's your partner?"

"A lady by the name of Lily Montgomery, and I don't reckon there's ever been a more beautiful, or for that matter, finer woman to come down the pike. Never mind that she runs a saloon. Ask anyone and they'll tell you, Lily is a fine woman."

A train whistle sounded down by the depot, and Langdon finished the rest of his drink in one swallow. "I've got to be goin'," he said. "That will be the last train to Barlow tonight. Will you fellows be comin'?"

"What's this Colonel Barlow look like?" Buck asked.

"Oh, he's a medium-size fellow," Langdon answered. "Dark brown hair, brown eyes."

"Does he have a scar, right here?"

Langdon's eyes widened. "Yes," he said. "Yes, he does. Do you know Colonel Barlow?"

"Yeah," Buck said. "I know him."

"Look here," Langdon said, nervously. "I hope I haven't talked out of turn. I mean, if..."

Lance held up his hand. "Mr. Langdon, you've done us a great service," he said. "I want to thank you." The train whistled again.

"Yes," Langdon said, still nervous. "Well, I suppose I'd better get going."

Buck and Lance watched Langdon hurry out the door.

"When do you want to go?" Buck asked.

Lance took another drink of his beer. "We can take our time now," he said. "It doesn't look to me like our man is going anywhere."

CHAPTER 7

THE MAIN STREET IN BARLOW RAN EAST and west, while the railroad ran north and south. The east and west orientation of the street was due to the fact that when the town, originally called Long Point, was built, its founders anticipated the coming of the Houston and Central Texas. The Houston and Central Texas would have run east and west, more in alignment with the street, but the Barlow railroad, approached the town from the north. Thus, the town was a giant X scratched out on the range floor, with the main street forming one leg of the X and the tracks the other.

Lance and Buck had spent the night in Brenham, then rode their horses down the next day. It took them about half-a-day of easy riding, so they arrived in the town at just about noon. The morning train down from Brenham had passed them no more than half- an-hour earlier, and now that same train, having been turned around by the rail loop, was standing at the depot, waiting to return to Brenham. As it stood there, its relief valves opened and closed every few seconds so that the rushing noise of the released steam filled the air like the heavy breathing of some serpentine monster.

There was quite a bit of activity around the depot...wagons loading and unloading, passengers getting on and off, citizens welcoming new arrivals or saying good-bye to travelers...but the main part of the town was quiet. Looking down the street the brothers could see that there were two buildings which stood out sharply. One was the Barlow Bank, which was of substantial construction, and the other was the Easy Pickin's Hotel and Saloon.

The bank was midway down the main street on the south side of the street. Directly across the street from the bank was the hotel and saloon. The Easy Pickin's was a frame building, two stories high and painted white, thus contrasting sharply with the rest of the buildings along the street, all of which were unpainted. A second-story balcony ran all the way around the outside of the hotel and below, facing the street, was a large wooden porch. There were half-a- dozen chairs on the porch and they were occupied by white-bearded old men who scarcely noticed when Buck and Lance rode up.

The brothers tied up at the hitching post, then went inside. There were more than two dozen patrons in the saloon, some standing at the bar and others sitting at tables. Buck and Lance stood just inside the door for a moment to let their eyes adjust to the dimmer light, then they stepped up to the bar.

The bar was made of burnished mahogany and it featured a highly polished footrail. Buck thought that was a little unusual for a saloon this far out. Most saloons had unfinished, rough-plank bars, and many didn't even have that, using instead, boards which were stretched across sawhorses. Whoever owned this bar took particular pride in maintaining a good place.

There were even crisp white towels hanging on hooks from the customers' side of the bar, spaced every four feet. A mirror was behind the bar and it was flanked on each side by small statues of nude women set back in special niches. A row of whiskey bottles sat in front of the mirror, reflected in the glass so that the row seemed to be two deep. A barkeep, with slicked black hair and a handlebar mustache, stood behind the bar, industriously polishing glasses.

"What will it be for you two gents?" he asked.

"Beer," Buck answered.

"Make it two," Lance put in.

The barkeep started to draw the two beers but a

very pretty young woman with copper-colored hair and a dark green silk dress, with a deep neckline, walked around behind the bar and put her hand on the spigot.

"I'll take care of these gentlemen, Fred," she said. Her voice was soft and cultured, with the hint of a Southern drawl.

The woman drew the two beers, then set the mugs in front of Buck and Lance, showing a generous amount of cleavage as she did so. She smiled at them, and her eyes danced with reflected light.

"Let me guess," she said. "You are Buck and Lance Chaney."

The brothers registered surprise at her calling them by name.

"How did you know?"

"You have to be the two gentlemen Jess told me about," the woman answered. "You're both handsome, and except for the difference in size, you look alike. He said you'd be coming down in a day or two."

"And you are Lily Montgomery," Lance said.

"At your service."

Lance smiled. "Mr. Langdon didn't deceive us when he told us how beautiful you are."

"Flattery will get you everywhere," Lily replied, smiling broadly. "Fred, these drinks are on the house."

Buck nodded thanks over the mug of his glass. He blew away some of the foam, then took a deep, thirsty swallow. It was as cool and refreshing as a mountain stream, and he drank the entire mug without putting it down.

Lily put another one in front of him and Buck picked it up and took another long drink before he set it down as well. He let out a sigh of contentment and brushed foam off his lips with the back of his hand.

"Quite a place you have here," Buck said, looking around the saloon.

A very pretty young girl came down the stairs and stopped at the far end of the bar. Fred, the bar-keep, went down to her and they talked quietly for a moment.

"The way Jess arid I look at it," Lily explained, "if we can only own one place in Barlow, then why not make it the best?"

"Make's sense to me," Buck replied. "But of course, the question that comes to mind is, why be here in the first place?"

"Why, Mr. Chaney, everyone has to be some-where," Lily answered.

"I agree," Buck said. "But that doesn't sound like a Texas drawl to me. I'd say it was more Mississippi or Alabama."

For just an instant, the sparkle died in Lily's eyes,

and though the smile never left her face, Buck could see way down, deep inside, and he regretted making the comment.

"I'm sorry, ma'am, I've already said too much," Buck apologized. "I reckon we all have things we'd as soon not remember."

Fred, who had been talking to the young girl at the end of the bar, came back to speak to Lily.

"It's Ann, Miss Lily. She says one of her customers is getting a little rough with her. He sent her down for a bottle of whiskey, but she's afraid to go back up."

"He hit me, Miss Lily," Ann said, and Buck noticed then that there was fresh red swelling on her cheek. "Do I have to go back?"

"No, of course you don't have to go back up," Lily said. "How much did he pay you?"

"He gave me a copper chit worth two dollars," the girl answered in a soft voice.

"Fred, give me two dollars from the till," Lily ordered.

Fred opened the cash drawer and gave Lily two dollars. She clinked the coins together in her hand, then started for the stairs. At about the time she reached the foot of the stairs a man, wearing only trousers, appeared at the railing on the upper balcony.

"Hey, you, girl!" he shouted down at Ann. "I sent

you down there to get me a bottle of whiskey, not have a quilting bee. You've been down there long enough! Get back up here!"

"I'm not coming back," Ann said.

"What? The hell you ain't. You better get back up here now, if you know what's good for you."

"I told her she doesn't have to come back up," Lily said.

"Say, isn't that—" Lance started, but Buck answered before the question was even asked.

"Yeah," he said. "That's Jack Wiggins, the same son of a bitch I threw off the train."

"He gets around, doesn't he?"

"What do you mean she's not comin' back up?" Wiggins demanded. "I paid for her, by God. She belongs to me."

"I have your money here," Lily said, holding up the silver so he could see it. "I'll be happy to return it to you as soon as you get dressed and leave."

"By God, I ain't goin' nowhere!" Wiggins shouted. It wasn't until that moment that anyone realized he was holding a gun. He raised the pistol and pointed it toward Lily. "Now, you tell that slut to get back up here," he said menacingly. "Otherwise, I'm going to put a bullet in that pretty face of yours."

"Wiggins," Buck shouted up to him. "Put the gun down."

Wiggins looked toward Buck, then recognized him. His face contorted with rage.

"You!" he shouted. He swung his gun toward Buck and fired. The bullet slammed into the bar between Buck and Lance. In one motion, Buck had his own gun out and he fired back just as Wiggins loosed a second shot.

Wiggins's second shot smashed into the mirror behind the bar, sending shards of glass all over the place but doing no further damage. He never got a third, because Buck made his only shot count.

Wiggins dropped his gun over the rail and it fell to the bar floor twelve feet below. He grabbed his neck and stood there, stupidly, for a moment, clutching his throat as bright red blood spilled between his fingers. Then his eyes rolled up in his head and he crashed through the railing, turned over once in midair, and landed heavily on his back alongside his dropped gun. He lay motionless on the floor with open but sightless eyes staring toward the ceiling. The saloon patrons who had scattered when the first shot was fired, began to edge toward the body. Up on the second floor landing a half-dozen girls and their customers, in various stages of dress and undress, moved to the smashed railing to look down on the scene.

Gunsmoke from the three charges had merged by now, and it formed a large, acrid-bitter cloud which drifted slowly toward the door. Beams of sunlight became visible as they stabbed through the cloud. There were rapid and heavy footfalls on the wooden sidewalk outside as more people began coming in through the swinging doors. One of the first ones in was a white-haired, heavyset man with a tired, defeated look to his eyes. As he passed through the sun bars, there was a flash of light from the star on his chest.

"What's the trouble here?" he asked, looking around the room.

One of the eyewitnesses chuckled.

"Ain't no trouble now, Marshal Chism. As usual, you're about a day late and a dollar short. This here fellow done took care of it."

"You the one who did the shootin'?" the marshal asked.

"Yes," Buck answered easily.

"Then you're under arrest, mister."

"What? Marshal Chism, have you lost what few brains you have? What are you arresting him for?"

"For the murder of Jack Wiggins."

"Hold on there, Marshal," Fred said. "You're making an awful big mistake here. This man had no choice. Wiggins commenced to shootin' first."

"That's the size of it, Marshal," one of the others agreed. "Fact is, he shot twice before this fellow shot once."

"That's right," still another confirmed.

"You arrest him, you're goin' to have every one of us as witnesses for the defense," still another patron put in.

"They're telling the truth, Marshal," Lily said. Marshal Chism sighed, then slipped his pistol back into his holster. He looked down toward the body. "I don't know," he said. "I'm not much lookin' forward to tellin' the Colonel that one of his men got himself kilt, and I didn't do nothin' about it."

"Try telling him it was self-defense," Lily suggested. "I'll try. I don't know that it'll do much good, but I'll try." The marshal looked up at the crowd. A couple of the more curious had even squatted beside Wiggins's body to get a closer look at it.

"Where you reckon all his silver is?" one of them asked.

"More than likely, up in the girl's room," another said.

"Marshal, I'll have Fred get his boots and belt buckle. If he has any family anywhere, it ought to go to them."

"All right," Chism said. He pointed to a couple of the men. "You two, get him over to Peterson's hardware store so Pete can get started on a coffin."

"You know the first question Peterson's goin' to ask, don't you, Marshal? He's goin' to want to know who's payin' for the buryin'.'"

"I'm goin' out to Gold Dust now. I reckon the Colonel will take care of his buryin'."

The two men Chism assigned to the job picked up the body, one under the shoulders, the other at the feet. Wiggins sagged badly in the middle and they had to struggle to carry him. A couple of the other patrons held open the swinging doors while the two men carried him out into the street.

"Miss Lily, I...I don't want to go back into my room till all his things is gone," Ann said.

"I'll get it taken care of," Lily offered. "Why don't you go on up to my room and lie down for a while?"

"Thanks," Ann said.

With the body gone, most of the customers returned to their own tables to discuss the shooting. It was played and replayed a dozen times over during the next few minutes, and though a couple of the men made some small comment to Buck, most left him alone. For that Buck was grateful. He had only Lance and Lily for company, and that was the way he wanted it.

A few minutes later Jess Langdon came into the saloon, and he walked right up to the bar and shook Buck's hand.

"I just heard what happened. You make quite an' entrance into town, young man," he said. He put out his hand toward the bar without even looking, knowing that his drink would be there and, indeed,

Fred had begun pouring it the moment he saw Jess come through the door. It was there, just as Fred knew it would be.

"This isn't exactly the entrance I would have chosen to make," Buck said. "But that fellow had a burr under his saddle and there was just no getting rid of it."

"It's just as well it happened the way it did," Jess said. "Jack Wiggins is the kind who would've waylaid you without so much as a second thought." Langdon saw that they were standing with Lily. "I see you met my Lily."

"Your Lily?" Lance asked.

"Yes," Jess said. He smiled and put his arm around her. "She's like a daughter to me. But if I were thirty years younger...hell, even if I were ten years younger I might..." He let the sentence trail off. "Believe me, the man who does lay claim to her will have to answer to me first," he went on.

"Don't worry, Jess," Lily laughed. "I'll see to it that you approve."

Jess smiled proudly, then looked back at the two brothers. "Where will you fellows be staying?"

"To be honest, we haven't given that much of a thought," Lance answered.

"Will you be looking for work?"

"Yes."

"Have you ever worked as a ranch hand?"

"Of course."

"Well, it's all settled, then. You can work for me. Come on out to the place today. I pay top dollar, I've got a really nice bunkhouse for my hands and there's plenty of room. Besides, I want you to come to a meeting tonight."

"A meeting?" Lily asked. "Jess, what's up?"

"I think you can guess, Lily," Jess answered. "I've invited all the other ranchers...that is, the ones who are still around...to come over tonight to discuss what we can do about Barlow. Seems he's just closed up another creek. That'll about do in the Hayes' place."

"We might be interested in coming to this meeting at that," Buck said. "Is Barlow going to be there?"

Jess chuckled. "I hardly think so."

"Too bad. I'm really anxious to meet that fellow," Buck said.

"Yes," Jess said. He rubbed the stubble on his cheek and peered at Buck and Lance through narrowed eyes, as if trying to size them up. "Now that I think of it, you two boys was askin' questions about him in Brenham. You even described him. Do you know him from somewhere?"

"If his name really is Barlow, we don't know him," Buck said.

"You mean you don't think that's his name."

"No."

"Well, we aren't that particular about folks' names out here," Jess explained. "Unless they give us reason to be particular. And I must confess, Barlow is giving us more and more reason to be curious."

"Who do you think Barlow is?" Lily asked.

"If he is who I think he might be, his name isn't Barlow. It's Armstrong," Buck said. "Samuel Armstrong."

"Actually, it is Samuel Barlow Armstrong," Lily said quietly.

"What?" Langdon said, looking at Lily in surprise. "See here, Lily. You mean you know this man? I mean, from somewhere else?"

"Yes," Lily said. "I knew him a long time ago."

"Why have you never said anything about it?"

"He knows me, too," Lily said. "I guess we both wanted to leave our past behind. Whatever he's done out here, I didn't figure his past had anything to do with it."

Jess looked at Buck and Lance. "But his past has something to do with what you want him for, right?"

"You might say that," Lance said.

"Wait a minute!" Jess suddenly said, holding up his finger in sudden recognition of the name. "Armstrong, you say? Samuel Armstrong? Wasn't he a guerrilla, like Quantrill?"

"That's right."

"I'll be damned. So he did fight in the war. I never did believe what he said about Gettysburg. My brother was there and nothing this Barlow fellow ever said agreed with anything my brother told me about that battle. Wonder why he would make up such a thing? There's folks around here who figure people like Armstrong and Quantrill and Anderson were as much heroes as people like Robert E. Lee or Stonewall Jackson."

"And there are others of us who think he wasn't fighting for the South at all. We think he was out for himself," Lance said.

"I get it," Jess said. "There's a price on his head, isn't there? Is that why you are out for him? You aim to collect the bounty?"

"No. No reward. Our reason is strictly personal."

"I see. I'm curious. Did you boys fight for the North or the South?"

"I fought for the South," Buck said. "My brother fought for the North."

Jess looked at them in surprise. "I'm sorry," he finally said. "It must have been particularly hard on you two, being on opposite sides like that."

"Yes, sir. But that war's over now," Lance said.

"That war?"

"Yes, sir, that war," Buck explained. "You see, our private war with Armstrong goes on."

"Well, boys, I must confess that it would make

things a heap nicer around here if somebody would take care of Colonel Barlow, or Armstrong, or whoever he is. But so far everything he has done has been strictly legal. It has been unethical perhaps, but legal, never the less. He's turned into a leading citizen, not only of Barlow, but of Texas. And right now, he has the law on his side. So, I'd be awfully careful about settling old scores, if I were you."

"We'll be careful enough. But we are going to settle things," Lance said.

"I think you also need to know that he spends practically all of his time out on the ranch, surrounded by armed men. He's not somebody you can just ride up and see."

"Besides that, he knows you two are coming after him," Lily put in. "And he knows you are here."

"How does he know?"

"He has a standing reward out for information on anyone new coming into town," Lily explained. "I always thought he was still worried about the price on his head from the war. Now I know it was you he was looking for. I don't know why you want him, but he is frightened of you. He is very frightened."

"He has a right to be," Lance answered ominously.

"Well, what about my offer?" Jess asked. "You're going to need someplace to hang your hat while you're going after Barlow. Will you come work for me?"

Lance smiled and took Jess's hand in his own. "Mr. Langdon, I'll be glad to work for you."

"That go for your brother, too?"

Lance chuckled. "I learned a long time ago, I can't speak for him."

"I'll be there," Buck said, reaching out to shake Jess's hand. "If for no other reason than to keep my clumsy brother from tearing up your place."

CHAPTER 8

AS THE WESTERN HILLS TURNED FROM RED to purple in the setting sun, Jess Langdon's friends and neighbors began arriving for the meeting. Wagons and buggies brought entire families across the range to gather at the Langdon house. Children who lived too far apart to play with each other were delighted with this unexpected opportunity, and they laughed and squealed and ran from wagon to wagon to greet their friends before dashing off to a game of kick-the-can. The women were equally pleased with the opportunity to visit and they brought cakes and pies from home, then gathered in the kitchen to make coffee, thus turning the business meeting into a great social event. Many of them brought quilts and they spread them out so that while the men were meeting, they could talk and work on the elaborate colors and patterns of the quilts they would be displaying at the next fair.

Buck and Lance met the other cowboys who were working for Langdon. Some of them had worked for ranchers who had lost their property to Colonel Barlow, and when the ranchers lost their property, the cowboys lost their jobs. Of course some of the cowboys went over to work for Barlow and Buck learned that some of the men who were now working for Langdon had once worked for Barlow.

To the average cowboy the differences between the ranchers didn't affect them. As long as there were cows to herd there would be a need for cowboys and they didn't particularly care who owned them.

That wasn't the case with all of them though, especially those who had worked for Barlow in the past and had left him because they didn't approve of some of his tactics.

Though the meeting was open to the hands as well as the ranch owners, the cowboys declined, respectfully, and stayed in the bunkhouse playing cards and keeping their own counsel. In fact, Buck hadn't really wanted to go either. He would have much preferred to stay back in the bunkhouse and get involved in the poker game some of the cowboys started. They attended the meeting though, because Lance reminded him that they were specifically invited by Langdon and it would have been impolite of them to refuse. What really convinced Buck to come, however, was when Lance suggested that they might hear something which would give them a lead on what Armstrong may have done with the gold.

The ranchers held their meeting in the parlor and Buck sat on a chair which had been brought over from the bunkhouse. So far he had heard nothing which related to the gold, so his interest in the conversation was waning. Buck tipped his chair back against the wall near the open window and watched the bugs flutter around a kerosene lantern which burned brightly on the nearby table.

"Gentlemen," Langdon was saying. "It's obvious that the situation is beginning to get quite serious."

"You ain't tellin' me nothin'," a big man answered. He pointed to two other men who were his same size, but much younger. "Me and my two boys here are goin' to have to sell off half our beeves for less money that it took to raise 'em, just 'cause we don't have water anymore. As you know, Barlow damned up Sweetwater Creek."

"Yeah. And because of that I've only got half the water I used to have," one of the other ranchers complained. "And to make matters worse, that damn Barlow's got me locked in. I can't even drive my cows to market without crossin' his land, and believe me, he plans to charge plenty for it."

"I know," a third put in. "The only way he'll let cows cross his land without chargin' a toll, is if we use his railroad to ship them. But he charges so much for freight that by the time you get to market, you can't make no money."

Langdon held up his hand.

"We could all tell stories like this," he said. "The point is, it's time we did something about it."

"Have you got something in mind?" the big man asked.

Langdon rubbed his hands together for a moment, then nodded toward Emerson Gray, who had been watching and listening to the whole thing. "I think Mr. Gray might have a suggestion or two," he said.

Emerson Gray was Lucinda's father, and Buck looked at him to see what he was like. He could see where Lucinda got her looks because Mr. Gray was a tall, handsome man. Gray had been sitting in a rocking chair and, at Jess's invitation, he stood up to address the other men who were gathered there.

"Men, there's not a one of us here, not even Jess Langdon or me, who is big enough to go up against Barlow alone. So here's my suggestion. We'll merge our cattle, our grass, and our water. Even with us all together, we won't be as big as Gold Dust, but at least we'll be more than he can chew off in one bite."

"So, what are you saying? You want to buy us out?" someone asked. "What's the difference between sellin' out to you and Langdon, or sellin' out to Barlow?"

"Miller's right. I come out here to do my own ranchin', and I'll be damned if I'm goin' to give it up without a fight," another put in. "I'm not ready to sell out to anyone yet."

"Now hold on there, Hayes, Miller," Gray said, holding up his hands to stop them. "You don't understand. I didn't say anything about you men selling out to us. We don't want to buy you out, and we couldn't afford it if we did. In the plan I'm suggesting, you'll still own your own cattle, and you'll still own your own land."

"Well, then how would somethin' like this work?" Hayes wanted to know.

"It's simple," Gray answered. "What we'll do is form the Greater Texas Cattle Company, and each of us will own a share of that company, proportionate to what we put in. And even though the cattle will have free access to the grass and water of any rancher who is a member of the company, we'll still keep title to our own land and possession of our own cattle. In fact, we'll even keep our own brands."

"What about the men it would take to work an outfit that size?" Miller asked. "Where would we get them? Most of us are runnin' our own spreads now with just a few hands, or no hands at all except for our own families. Looks to me like the way you're settin' this up, those of us that don't have any hands will be workin' for the company."

"That's right, Mr. Miller," Langdon said, standing to join Gray. "You will be working for the company. But don't forget, you are the company. Therefore, you'd be working for yourself, just as you are now."

"It's all well and good to say we are the company, but when it comes right down to it, somebody's goin' to have to be the boss, right?"

"Yes, of course," Langdon replied. "We'd have anarchy otherwise."

"I don't know. I don't hold much luck with workin' for someone else."

At that the big man with the two sons stood up and looked at the others.

"Well, by God, I'll work for a boss," he said. "I don't like workin' for the other fellow any more than any of you do. But the way I look at it, if I do this, at least I'm goin' to have a piece of the pie we're bakin' up here. Besides, if we don't do somethin' soon, Barlow's goin' to wind up with the whole damned thing and we will all either be workin' for the son of a bitch, or we'll have to leave here."

"Thank you, Jim," Jess said.

The big man looked over at Jess. "Jess, you can put Jim Simpson and both my boys down as joinin' you. We don't have no hands except ourselves, but we'll start workin' as soon as you want us."

"Anyone else?" Jess asked.

"All right," Hayes finally relented. "If Jim can go along with this, then I reckon I can, too. I'll come over, and I'll bring both my hired hands with me."

"Me, too," Miller said. "I got no hired hands and no kids. There's just me and my wife, but if that's enough for you, we'll be glad to work for the company."

"Of course you and your wife are enough. Every hand counts, Paul," Emerson Gray said.

"All right, as long as you're countin', count me in," another rancher added.

Within a few moments every man in the room had agreed to become partners in the Greater Texas Cattle Company.

"Good, good," Jess said, smiling happily at their decision. "Gentlemen, I predict things are going to change for the better around here. Now, I declare the Greater Texas Cattle Company is formed. Our next piece of business is to elect a president, and I nominate Emerson Gray."

"Emerson's got my vote," someone else said, and the support proved so overwhelming for Emerson Gray that no one else was even nominated.

"Thank you," Emerson said. "Now, let's get down to business."

Buck listened to the details of organization for a while, but he eventually grew bored and, quietly, let himself out of the room. He stood for a few moments on the long porch which stretched all the way across the front of the Langdon house, listening to the bugs thump softly against the muslin screens which covered the windows and the front door. He looked up at the stars which filled the night with their diamond brilliance, then, after a moment of studying the stars, glanced over toward a line of cottonwood trees which were waving gently in the evening breeze. As the trees moved back and forth, the branches of one of them gathered some of the moon's soft light and sent slivers of silver through the night.

The trees were along the bank of a small but swiftly flowing river which cut through the middle of Langdon's ranch. The river supplied water year-round and kept Jess Langdon independent of Barlow's dams and diversions. The question Buck and Lance had both asked themselves when they learned of Jess's proposal to pool the herds was, would the river supply enough water for everyone?

In all honesty, Buck and Lance didn't think it would. They thought Jess was taking quite a chance by inviting the others in. His proposal was that, united, they would have more strength. United they may have more strength, but they would also use up the resources more quickly. It was a risk Jess was willing to take, however, and both Buck and Lance admired him for that.

Buck saw a young woman standing at the edge of the river, looking down at the water. He knew that it was Lucinda Gray and as he had not seen her since the incident on the train, he decided to walk down to talk to her. Her back was to him so she didn't notice him until he was almost to her.

"Hello, Miss Gray," Buck said.

Lucinda turned at the sound of his voice, then, recognizing him as her onetime benefactor, she smiled at him.

"Hello, Mr. Chaney," she replied.

"You remembered my name," Buck replied. "I'm flattered."

"Of course I remember it. Besides, after what happened in town today, your name is on everyone's lips."

"Oh. I guess you mean the business with Wiggins. That's not exactly the way I'd like to be known."

"I'm glad you weren't hurt," Lucinda went on.

"Well, thanks," Buck said. He smiled. "I guess I'm sort of glad of that, myself."

Lucinda pointed toward the house. The door and windows were glowing brightly with the golden light of many candles and lanterns.

"Don't you think what's going on in there is wonderful?" she asked.

"Wonderful?"

"Yes. If we would all just stick together, we could beat Colonel Barlow and make this a decent place for everyone."

Buck laughed.

"Why are you laughing?"

"You make it sound like the beginning of a crusade."

"Suppose I do? Is there anything wrong with that?"

"No, no, of course not," Buck said quickly. "I didn't mean anything by my remark."

Lucinda wrapped her arms around herself. "Oh, it's at times like this that I wish I were a man."

Buck made a clicking sound with his tongue and he shook his head. "No, ma'am," he said. "I like you just the way you are."

"But I'm missing out on everything. If I were a man I could be right in there with them. Why are you out here? Why aren't you inside where all the excitement is?"

Buck chuckled softly, then put his hands, gently, on her shoulders. "Because I think it's a lot more exciting to be out here with a beautiful girl," he replied. He kissed her, and was surprised to find that she didn't try to fight him. When the kiss was over he looked at her, and his eyes reflected his curiosity.

"I know what you are thinking," she said, answering his unasked question. "You are wondering why I'm not acting shocked, and making a big thing about you kissing me. Well, I suppose I should but the truth is, I liked it. And if I liked it, why should I act so silly about it? Men don't act silly about a little kiss, do they?"

"No," Buck said, smiling at her response. "No, I don't guess we do."

Well, I'm as good as any man," Lucinda went on. "I can ride as well as anyone on my dad's ranch. I can shoot as well, too. So, if I want to let you kiss me, then I should have the right to do that, don't you agree?"

"Oh, yes, of course, I agree," Buck said, still surprised by her action but definitely wanting to encourage it.

"But," Lucinda said, holding up a finger in warning. "Don't think that means I'll hold still for anything else, Buck Chaney, because I won't. So don't try and force me into anything."

"Oh, no, I wouldn't think of trying anything like that," Buck promised. "I'm just…" Buck stopped in midsentence and stared off toward the horizon. He saw the orange glow of what had to be a rather large fire, and he pointed it out to Lucinda. "Lucinda, are there any houses over that way?"

"Yes, that's where the Millers…Buck! Their house! It's on fire!"

Buck ran back toward the house. Inside, the ranchers were still discussing the details of the organization and they looked up when Buck burst into the room.

"Quick!" Buck shouted. "The Miller house is on fire!"

In the east the sun had risen full disk. A dozen wagons were parked in the soft morning light, and in the wagons, nestled among quilts and blankets, slept the children of the families who had come, first to the gathering at the Langdon ranch, and then to help fight the fire. The light of day now disclosed the damage the fire had done. The Miller house was completely destroyed. So was the smokehouse and the granary. Only the barn had been saved, and that, through the prodigious effort of all who had come to help.

Marva Miller stood in her husband's arms, weeping softly. The Millers, like everyone else out here, were covered with soot and ash from the blackened ruins of their home. On the ground under a tree, sat a pitiful pile of what belongings they had managed to pull from the ashes. Most of their belongings were ruined, burned and twisted beyond recognition. Here and there, however, a few things had survived the flames, and their bright undamaged colors shined incongruously from the pile of blackened rubble.

Everyone was tired and covered with a great sadness, for the death of a home was particularly hard in an area where homes and people were few and far between.

Buck walked over to the well and lowered one of the buckets they had used in their unsuccessful fire brigade. He brought up a bucket of water then dipped the tin dipper in for a drink. He saw Lance walking toward him, carrying a burned, rusted tin container.

"What's that?" Buck asked.

"It's the culprit, I'm afraid. It's coal oil," Lance replied. Lance looked over toward Miller. "Mr. Miller?"

Miller looked up. His eyes were red-rimmed and everyone was willing to grant him the pretense that his red eyes were caused by the fire and the smoke.

"Yes?" Miller responded.

"Mr. Miller, did you have a container of coal oil on the place?"

"Yes, I kept coal oil for the lanterns," Miller answered.

"Where did you keep it?"

"Out in the barn. Marva was afraid of the stuff."

"Is this it?" Lance asked, holding the burned, bent can out toward Miller.

"Yes, it is," Miller answered. He looked at the can, then over toward the barn. "That's funny," he said. "How could that be burned without the barn bein' burned?"

"I didn't find it in the barn," Lance replied. He pointed to the rear of what had been the house. "I found it over there, behind your house."

Gently, Miller pulled away from his wife's arms, then walked over to look at the can.

"Damn," he said. "That's the can, all right. And you say you found it over behind the house?"

"Yes, sir."

"But how can that be? I know I kept that can in the barn. In fact, I was going to refill the lanterns yesterday, but I never got around to it."

"I'll tell you how it can be," one of Simpson's sons put in. He was standing a little way from the rest of them, looking down at the ground. "We didn't notice this before, because it was too dark. But now that the sun's up, I can see tracks here, Mr. Miller. Tracks of a dozen horses or more. And they lead off that way, toward Gold Dust Ranch."

"Barlow!" Miller said in a choked voice. "That son of a bitch burned my home! I'm going to kill him!"

"Paul, no!" Marva shouted when she saw him start toward his wagon. "Somebody stop him, please!" Buck sprinted toward the wagon and he grabbed the team.

"Mr. Miller, you don't want to do this," he said. "If you go in there like this you'll only get yourself killed. Do you want to leave your wife a widow, as well as homeless?"

"What am I supposed to do?" Miller asked angrily. "Am I supposed to just stand around while he destroys everything I've built?"

"He hasn't destroyed everything," Jess put in quickly.

"What do you mean?" Miller replied. He swept his arm out across the burned residue of his home. "What do you call this?"

"He may have destroyed your house and a few belongings, Paul," Jess said. "But that's all. Your land is still here, your cattle are still in the field, and you still have friends."

"Yes," Simpson said. "We'll stick by you, Paul."

Miller sighed. "I thank you," he said. "But there's nothing left for us here, now. I reckon we'll just head on back East."

"You don't need to do that, Miller," Hayes said. "If you'll stay on here, tomorrow, we'll get started on a new house. Right, men?"

"Right," someone answered.

"And we've got a bed we can spare," one of the women added.

"And I have a sofa you can have," another woman put in.

Within moments, plans were made to rebuild and refurnish the Miller home, and now Marva's tears of sorrow had changed to tears of happiness, not only that her home would be restored, but that she and her husband were blessed with such friends.

"You're welcome to stay over at my house until yours is rebuilt," Jess offered.

Paul Miller embraced his wife and looked out over the smoke-blackened faces of his friends. His eyes glistened with tears, but this time he made no effort to hide them. These were tears of happiness.

"Thank you," he said. "But they didn't bum the barn. Marva and I can stay here until we get the house built again."

"Then that means you'll stay?"

"Yes," Miller said, smiling. "We'll stay."

Everyone cheered Miller's decision and, with plans to return the next day to start building, they began to leave, to return to their own homes.

Buck watched them leave, then he climbed onto his horse which was being held for him by Lance, who had already mounted.

"Lance, what are we waiting for?" Buck asked. "Let's go out there and get that son of a bitch now."

"Not so fast, little brother. If he really is surrounded by as many men as they say, we wouldn't get within half-a-mile of him before we were ambushed."

"I don't intend to go much longer before I settle this," Buck said. "If ever there was a man who needed killing, it's Samuel Barlow Armstrong."

***

Clay Beekman lay awake in the early morning light. Sleeping in the bed beside him was a girl he knew only as Elsie. She had seemed so young and pretty when he first saw her in a Brenham saloon two weeks ago. Now she looked old to him. Old and broken-down. She needed a bath and she was drooling through open slack lips which moved slightly as she snored.

Carl had already grown tired of her and was wanting to get rid of her. And now, as Clay looked at her this morning, he realized that he was tired of her, too. Today they would get rid of her. They would go up to Brenham, or maybe even as far as Hempstead, and find someone else.

That was one good thing he and Carl had going for them. They always had a woman around and when they got tired of her, they would simply get rid of her and get another one. And why not? They had enough money for it.

They never bothered to get two women. They were perfectly willing to share one and it never seemed to matter to the woman. Most of them were "on the line as Soiled Doves," when the Beekmans found them anyway, and if they didn't come with the Beekmans, then they often wound up with as many as ten or fifteen men in one night. Having to deal with just two men was a welcome respite for them, especially if they got as much money from the two as they did from fifteen regulars. With Clay and Carl they were assured of that, because the Beekmans always paid well. The Beekmans were generous that way. After all, that was what money was for.

Armstrong wasn't like that. In fact, if there was one question they could ask Armstrong, it would be why didn't he use his money for fun? What was the use in having it, if it didn't bring pleasure? It seemed like all Armstrong was interested in was buying land, and then more land. He wanted power and position, but what good was that if he didn't enjoy life?

Clay got up and walked through the house to the back porch. It was a nice house...not as large as the main house of course, but certainly nice enough for anything he and his brother might ever want. It was supposed to be the foreman's house, but the man who actually served as foreman of the ranch lived in the bunkhouse with the other hands.

Neither Clay nor Carl acted as foreman of the ranch. In fact, they did no ranching at all. They didn't have to. Though none of the hands knew it, Clay and Carl were actually partners with Armstrong in this operation. They weren't full partners, at least, not to the degree that they had any say in the operation of the ranch. But that didn't matter. They would rather let Armstrong run it anyway. They didn't like to fool with the day-to-day business of running a ranch, and it was obvious that Armstrong did.

If Clay and Carl did no actual ranch work, they did help out by taking care of other things. Like last night, for example.

Clay smelled his hands. They still smelled of smoke. He took a washbasin over to the pump and pumped up some water, then, using lye soap, washed away the smell.

Clay thought of the night before. In a way, it was like it had been during the war. He had burned several houses during the war and he discovered then that he actually enjoyed it. He remembered burning a house one night while the family stood out front screaming and crying as the flames consumed their home. It had excited him, like a woman excites him, and later that same night, he had raped a young girl.

Last night, as they rode away from the Miller place with the flames snapping and popping, and sparks riding the heat waves up a hundred feet or more, he had felt that same sense of sexual excitement. Although Armstrong told them beforehand that the Millers wouldn't be there, Clay had secretly hoped that the woman would be there. He would have taken her...taken her while she screamed and while the house burned. And it would have been fine. Oh, it would have been so fine.

She wasn't there, though. No one was there, so there was nothing to do except take out his terrible lust on Elsie when they got back to the ranch. Elsie didn't understand the ferocity with which Clay attacked her last night. After all, she told him, she was willing to give him anything he wanted. Why was he being so rough?

Elsie just didn't understand. He didn't want her to give him anything he wanted. He wanted to take it from her. He tried to rape her. It wasn't actually a rape, of course, because she was a willing participant, but, under the circumstances, it was as close as he could get. It did take the edge off his terrible need, but it didn't totally satisfy him.

Clay finished washing his face and hands, then he tossed the water out. He took a shirt off the back porch clothesline. This was one of the shirts that had belonged to Jack Wiggins. Yesterday, as soon as Clay heard about Wiggins getting himself killed, he went over to the bunkhouse and cleaned out Wiggins's belongings. None of Wiggins's silver was there, but he did have two nice shirts, and Clay took both of them.

Armstrong said Wiggins was killed by Buck Chaney. The fact that Buck Chaney had found them, frightened Armstrong. It didn't frighten Clay. If it was up to him he would just wait until he got the opportunity, then shoot Buck Chaney in the back. He never liked the son of a bitch anyway. Armstrong was trying to be respectable though, so he wouldn't go along with that. Clay believed the time might come, however, when Armstrong would regret not listening to him.

"Clay? Clay, honey, is that you out there on the back porch?" Elsie called.

"Yeah," Clay answered.

"Why don't you come on back in here, honey?" Elsie said. "Why don't you come on in here and get back in bed for a while?"

"Why don't you shut up?" Clay replied, tucking his shirt tail in as he walked away from the house.

Late in the afternoon of that same day, Samuel Barlow Armstrong was down at the pen where he kept his special blooded Hereford stock. He had one hundred head of the finest stock in the country, and his dream was to, eventually, have a herd of thousands of Herefords.

Most of the cattle herds in Texas consisted of longhorns, put together by ranchers who had built their herds by conducting "cow hunts." During, and right after the war, there had been great, roaming herds of cattle all over Texas. These wild herds, created from the old Spanish ranches, and from the prewar Texas herds, were so neglected during the war that they ran free and began to multiply.

Armstrong also had longhorns of course, but he knew that Herefords brought more on the market and he believed that the Hereford breed was the cow of the future.

Armstrong turned away from his contemplation at the stock pen, and was shocked to see that there was, and probably had been for some time, a man standing there looking at him. The man was tall and gaunt, with coal black hair and a neatly trimmed beard and mustache. His eyes were dark and penetrating.

"What the—" Armstrong asked, shocked by the sudden, and unexpected appearance. "Who the hell are you?" he asked. "How did you get here?"

"Shardeen," the man said in one word. The word slipped out like an escaping sigh.

Shardeen. Yes, Armstrong remembered now. He had heard of Shardeen the last time he was in Hempstead. It was said that Shardeen was the deadliest man with a gun in Texas. It was said, also, that he would hire out to anyone who could meet his price. One was warned, however, not to hire Shardeen unless they were serious, because death followed him wherever he went.

Armstrong was serious. He was too far into his dream to turn back now. If he had to get a little more ruthless to realize final success, then he would do it. Shardeen seemed like the solution to his problem, so he sent for him.

"Oh, yes," Armstrong said. He smiled and stuck out his hand, but Shardeen's hand stayed by his side. "Uh, yes," Armstrong said again, letting his hand fall awkwardly. "I did send for you. I want you to work for me."

"How much?"

"Five hundred dollars a month."

"That's a lot of money. You must have a lot of killing to do."

"Oh, if it all works out, it won't be necessary to do any killing," Armstrong said.

"There will be killing," Shardeen said, coldly. "That's what I do. Do you want me, or not?"

"I, uh..." Armstrong said, hesitating. Then he thought of the Chaney brothers. He hadn't even considered them when he first sent for Shardeen, because he didn't know they were around to constitute a danger to him. Now it seemed like an omen. They showed up and Shardeen showed up at the same time. With a man like Shardeen around, he needn't fear the Chaneys, no matter what they might do. "Yes," he said. "I want you. You can put your things in the bunkhouse."

"No, thanks," Shardeen said. He climbed onto his horse.

"No? You mean you won't work for me?"

"I'll work for you," Shardeen said. "But I won't stay in the bunkhouse."

"Where will you stay?"

"Around," Shardeen hissed.

"But how will I get hold of you if I need you?" Sam asked.

"You already did," Shardeen said. He clicked at his horse then rode away as quietly as he had appeared. As Armstrong watched him ride away, he shivered once. When he was young he used to believe that meant someone had just stepped on his grave.

CHAPTER 9

LUCINDA GRAY THOUGHT IT WAS A WONDERFUL thing the way everyone pitched in to help rebuild the Miller house. It took two weeks to get the job done, and those two weeks were the happiest two weeks in Lucinda's entire life. She knew it was no secret why she was so happy. During that time she was spending several hours each day with Buck Chaney, and she had fallen in love with him.

Of course, Lucinda was sorry the house had burned in the first place. She knew that the Millers had lost treasured old family heirlooms which could never be replaced, and her heart had gone out to them on that terrible night. She had cried bitter tears over their sorrow, but out of that sorrow had come the fellowship of everyone on the range working together, and out of it, too, had come a new awareness of herself.

Lucinda had always believed it was a cruel trick of fate that she had been born a woman in what she considered to be a man's world. She had always prided herself on her ability to ride and shoot like a man, and she believed that she even thought like a man.

Until she met Buck.

From the moment Lucinda Gray met Buck Chaney, things began to change. Now Lucinda was fully aware of the fact that she was a woman. And what's more, she was enjoying that awareness. When she was around Buck he made her feel things she had never before felt. When he touched her, or sometimes just when he spoke to her, she felt tingly all over. It was unlike anything she had ever experienced before...but it was a feeling she enjoyed.

For the first time in her life, Lucinda began to think about what it would be like to be married, and have a family. She suddenly realized that she wanted to have children...Buck's children, and she wanted to hold them in her arms.

The trouble was, Buck wasn't a man to speak his mind... if indeed, he even shared those feelings. Buck was a man who was consumed by some secret drive. Lucinda knew that he had suffered some great personal tragedy...and she knew that it had something to do with Colonel Barlow...a man Buck called Armstrong. The personal tragedy which affected Buck also affected his brother, Lance, and they were united in that. But there was something else. There was something beneath the tragedy that separated the brothers...though in a strange paradox, even that secret, whatever it was, held them together.

On the evening of the day they finished rebuilding the Miller house, Lucinda showed Buck a basket lunch she had prepared. She invited him to go with her down to a secret place she knew about on the bank of the river under a growth of poplar trees. There, she knew, was a soft, cool cushion of grass, and, because of a cut in the riverbank and the close-growing stand of trees, a place of absolute privacy. Lucinda brought a blanket with her and when they reached her secret place she spread the blanket out on the grass for their picnic.

The breeze was cooler coming off the river, and the leaves of the trees rustled pleasantly in the wind. In the west, the sun was slowly sinking in a brilliant display of color. Indian paintbrush, oxeyes, and daisies waved in colorful profusion on the opposite side of the river. Water broke white over polished rocks, and a trout jumped high, sparkled in rainbow colors, then splashed back into the stream.

After the meal of cold chicken and potato salad, Lucinda cleared off the blanket, then sat close to him. They talked of pleasant things, and though Lucinda laughed often, she was actually paying mere lip service to the conversation. What she really wanted to do was tell Buck she loved him and beg him to marry her. But such things simply weren't done, and in frustration and anger over things being the way they were, she began to cry.

Buck was surprised by Lucinda's totally unexpected reaction to what had been such a pleasant evening, and he looked at her with shock etched on his face.

"What is it?" he asked in surprise. "Lucinda? What is wrong?"

"What's wrong? Are you so dumb, Buck Chaney, that you can't see what's wrong?"

Buck looked at her blankly.

"Don't you have the slightest idea?" she asked.

"No," Buck replied truthfully.

"I'll tell you what's wrong. It's you and me and... and…" Lucinda started, but she couldn't hold back the hot tears and they began flooding so that it was impossible for her to continue. She lost all control then and cried without stopping.

Buck, in an attempt to comfort her, put his arms around her and drew her to him. He held her against him for a long moment until the tears abated.

Lucinda took an intense pleasure in that moment, bittersweet though it was. For a short while it was as if she really did belong to him. She would give anything if it was true.

***

A few days later, the two Simpson brothers, Arnold and Tom, were riding along the bank of a dried-up creek. Although the creek was not a year-round source of water for the Simpson place, it did normally have water at this time of the year and they were investigating why it had suddenly dried up.

They followed the dry creek bed all the way to the property line which divided the Simpson spread from Gold Dust and there, not fifty yards across the line, on the property of Gold Dust, they saw that a rock dam had been built. The dam stopped the flow of water and the precious water which, normally, would have flowed onto the Simpson ranch, was now backing up into a rather substantial pond, spreading out on Gold Dust land. Here was clearly an act of water piracy. At least, that was the opinion of the two Simpson brothers.

Arnold and Tom were both big men, well over six feet tall, and, because of their size, weren't used to doing things cautiously. As soon as they discovered the pile of rocks which interrupted the flow of their water, they grew angry. Without a second thought, they knocked down the fence that separated the properties, then went over to the newly constructed dam and began throwing the rocks out of the stream so that the water could flow again.

They had been working for about fifteen minutes or more when a stranger rode up, approaching them from deep within the acres of Gold Dust. The stranger was tall and gaunt looking, with black hair, and a mustache and goatee. His dark eyes, rather deeply set, were as cold and menacing as the eyes of a snake. He slid off his horse and walked over toward the creek where the two men were busily moving rocks.

"May I inquire," he began in a low, hissing voice, "as to what you men are doing?"

"Well, now, just what the hell does it look like, mister?" Tom replied angrily. "We're tearing down this dam."

"Would you put it back the way it was, please?" the man asked calmly.

"Like hell, we will. Who the hell are you to be telling us to put it back, anyway?"

"The name is Shardeen," the man answered in the same hissing voice.

"Shardeen, is it? Well, I've never heard of you, Mr. Shardeen."

"I'm going to ask you one more time to please put the rocks back," Shardeen said.

Arnold looked at the man. Neither he nor Tom had ever encountered a real killer before. They had no idea what to look for in the eyes, or the set of the mouth of a man who was prepared to kill, so they were not able to see it in this man. They viewed everyone and everything in terms of brute strength, and as neither of them had ever encountered anyone who was as strong as they were, they never knew the meaning of the word fear. Consequently, they felt no fear now.

"No dried-up little runt is goin' to tell me or my brother what to do...let alone that we got to put these rocks back," Arnold growled. "Now, get back on your horse and get the hell out of here before I break every bone in your runty little body."

Shardeen drew and fired twice. It happened so quickly that neither Tom nor Arnold ever realized they were in danger. They died, still defiant and still unafraid.

Shardeen looked down at the bodies of the two men he had just killed and, without a flicker of emotion in his dead flat eyes, rode away and left them.

A couple of hours later Shardeen returned with Marshal Chism to show him the two bodies he had "found" while riding fence for Colonel Barlow, his employer.

When Marshal Chism halted the wagon, he looked toward Simpson's house. In the back of the wagon, wrapped in canvas, lay the bodies of Jim Simpson's two sons. This wasn't a moment he was looking forward to.

The wagon tilted under Chism's weight when he

stepped down. As he started toward the house the front door opened and Jim Simpson and his wife stepped out onto the porch.

"Mornin', Marshal," Simpson said. He was rolling his shirtsleeves up, exposing massive forearms. "What can I do for you?"

"Mr. Simpson," Chism said. He paused, then took out his handkerchief and wiped his forehead. "I'm afraid I have some sad news to report."

"Sad news? What sort of sad news?"

"It's about your boys, Mr. Simpson." Chism cleared his throat, then pointed to the wagon. "I have them here."

Simpson looked toward the wagon and noticed, for the first time, the form under the canvas.

"Tom! Arnold!" Mrs. Simpson screamed, and she ran to the wagon and began pulling at the canvas, crying and calling her sons' names over and over. "What happened?" Simpson asked.

"They've been shot, Mr. Simpson."

"Shot? How? Where? Marshal, my boys were good boys. I know they didn't get shot in some saloon. Now, where did you find them?"

"One of Colonel Barlow's riders found them...on Gold Dust land," Chism said.

"Found them? Or murdered them?"

"Mr. Simpson, all I know is that he came to me and told me he had found two bodies. When I went out to investigate, I saw your two boys, both shot dead. I've no idea who did it."

"The hell you don't! It was Barlow! You know that as well as I do!"

"I don't know that, Mr. Simpson. In fact, as I said, it was one of Barlow's men who found them in the first place. He didn't have to report it, you know. He was just being a good neighbor, that's all."

"Good neighbor," Simpson said. He started toward the canvas-wrapped bodies. "He murdered my two boys, and you call him a good neighbor?"

"I'll help you," Marshal Chism offered.

"I don't need your help," Simpson said sharply, reaching for the first of his two sons. "My wife and me, we'll take care of our own." He pulled him off the wagon and laid him on the ground, then went back for the other. Then, when both boys were lying on the ground under a shade tree, he pulled his wife to him and held her for a long, silent moment.

"What are you going to do now, Mr. Simpson?" Chism asked.

"I'm going to bury my boys," Simpson said.

"If there is anything..."

"Just go. Leave us in peace," Simpson said.

Chism sighed, then snapped the reins and started the team back to town.

Two weeks after the funeral there were still no leads, and the Simpsons were officially listed as killed by person or persons unknown. Jim Simpson didn't leave the company, but without his sons to share with him, his participation in the Greater Texas Cattle Company was without spirit or enthusiasm.

Despite Jim Simpson's personal tragedy, the other cattlemen began rallying to the Cattle Company. Emerson Gray suggested that they gather their herds and have a cattle drive to Hempstead, thus boycotting Barlow's railroad. Everyone agreed wholeheartedly, so the cattle were brought together and plans were made for the drive.

Buck and Lance drew nighthawk duty a few nights before they were due to begin the drive, and they were sitting around the campfire, just after dark. The fire had burned down so that the flickering flames were gone, and there remained only the glowing red and orange of the embers. An open can of beans sat on a flat rock near the fire and a small wisp of steam curled from the top. Lance and Buck sat near the fire waiting for the beans to warm. Buck leaned over to look into the can.

"Looks like it's about ready," he said. "We'll cut up a pepper or two and it'll be a fine meal."

"It's a hell of a long way from being a fine meal, no matter what you do to it," Lance answered.

Out in the darkness a calf, separated from the others by a casual shifting of the herd, bawled in fright, to be answered by the reassuring call of its equally anxious mother.

"Hell, I didn't say I'd cook great meals for you, Lance. I just said I'd ride nighthawk with you," Buck said with a chuckle. Buck took a spoonful of beans. "Oh, I love them! They're great!" he said with exaggerated gusto.

Lance held out his plate and Buck spooned half the can onto it. Lance took a mouthful, then made a face.

"I'll tell you one thing, little brother. If you really do like this, you sure as hell are easy to please. If you ever get married, your wife won't have to be a very good cook to please you."

"Yeah," Buck said. "But, I don't have any plans for marriage right now."

"Oh?" Lance teased. "The way you and Lucinda been makin' eyes at each other, I was sort of thinkin' you might be gettin' married just any time. You could do worse than to settle down to ranching."

"Lucinda is a wonderful woman," Buck said. "I only wish I was worthy of her. If I thought—" Suddenly, Buck stopped in midsentence and cocked his ear to listen. "What was that?" he asked.

Both men had heard it about the same time. It was a quiet sound, a subtle sound which the average person would have never discerned, but which stood out sharply to the senses of the two men. It was the sound of horses' hooves, as distinguished from the sound of the hooves of thousands of milling cattle.

"Jess didn't say anything about a relief rider tonight, did he, Lance?" Buck asked.

"No, he didn't," Lance answered, and the beans were tossed aside as both men moved quickly toward their rifles.

Lance jacked a round into his rifle, then made a silent motion with his hand to send Buck around one side, while he started around the other. Both men moved stealthily through the night, headed toward the sound of the intruder.

Lance ran through the darkness, crouched low, watching the ground before him in the dim moonlight so that he wouldn't trip. Off to his right was the low, large mass of cattle, the combined herds of all the ranchers. Beyond the herd lay the quiet, restless range, and beyond that, a distant, timeless line of hills. The hills blocked out the horizon so that it was impossible to see in silhouette anyone who might be sneaking around.

Lance followed the creek up to a higher elevation until he reached a rock outcropping about three-quarters of the way up the draw. He lay flat on the rocks and looked out over the herd. It was difficult to see anything more than a large, black mass.

"Lance! Two men toward Snake Butte!" Buck

suddenly yelled. A flash of fire and a rifle shot followed Buck's call, and Lance knew that his brother had fired on the two men.

The rifle shot startled the two horsemen into activity and they both left at a gallop. Their sudden movement and the sound of their horses alerted Lance to their presence and he, too, fired at them, not really trying to hit either one of them, but merely trying to spur their retreat on.

Neither of the two riders returned fire, and, as they were leaving rapidly, neither Lance nor Buck risked a second shot, lest they stampede the herd. Lance hurried back down the creek bank until he returned to the campfire. He had gone farther than Buck, so Buck was already there by the time Lance returned.

"Did you see them?" Buck asked.

"Yeah," Lance answered. "I wonder who they were and what they were doing here."

"They were cattle thieves," Buck said. "They'd already cut two out of the herd and were trying to get away with them."

"Two? You mean they took that risk for just two cows?"

"That's all they had with them," Buck replied. "Maybe they were just cutting them out for food."

"I don't know, that sounds awfully strange, don't you think?"

"It does a little," Buck admitted. Buck picked up his saddle and started toward his horse.

"Where are you going?"

"To pick up the two beeves. They're just standing out there where the rustlers left them."

"You mean they aren't returning to the herd?"

"No."

"That's odd," Lance said. Lance picked up his own saddle.

"What are you doing?" Buck asked.

"I'm going with you," Lance said. "There's something funny going on here, and I want to see what it is."

A moment later Buck and Lance approached the two cows. One of them was lying on the ground and the other one was walking with a peculiar gait which made it draw up first one foot and then the other as it moved.

"What? What the hell is that?" Buck asked. "Those cows are sick."

"Son of a bitch!" Lance swore. He leaped from his saddle and moved quickly over to the cow. He looked at its mouth, then kneeled beside the animal to look at its hooves. On the skin, just above the hooves, there were dozens of blisters.

"Lance, what is it?"

"Hoof-and-mouth disease!" Lance said.

"My God!" Buck exclaimed. "They weren't stealing the cattle, they were bringing them in! They were trying to infect the herd!"

"It looks that way," Lance said. Lance pulled his pistol.

"What are you going to do?"

"We have to shoot them and burn them, right now."

"Don't you think we should let Jess and the others see them first?"

"No," Lance answered. "We can't take a chance on the herd getting infected. We need to destroy them as quickly as possible."

"All right," Buck said. He pulled his own pistol. "Let's get it done."

"You were correct to destroy them right away," Jess said, as he and half-a-dozen other owners stood around the little pile of charred bones...all that remained of the two cows.

"You're certain they had no contact with the other animals?" Hayes asked.

"I'm positive," Lance replied. "We heard them as they were coming up and we chased them off before they could introduce their cows to the herd. When we came back to look at the two cows we saw they were diseased so we killed them."

"I want to hear how Barlow gets out of this," Miller said angrily.

"Same as he did with killing my boys," Simpson said. "Same as he did with burning your house. He'll deny knowing anything about it and, of course, without proof, what can we do?"

"We have to do something," Miller said angrily. "We can't just let this go on."

"I have an idea," Lance suggested. "Why don't we give the cows back to him?"

"What do you mean? You killed them."

"He doesn't know that," Lance said. "We could cut a couple out of the herd that look just like the two we killed, then get Marshal Chism to ride along with us while Buck and I put the animals back in his herd. That would be the neighborly thing to do, don't you think?"

Jess smiled broadly. "If he thinks they are the contaminated animals...my God! He'll go crazy!"

"You know," Lance said, "a little lye water on the hooves and mouths of a few of his cows might even help him along."

Buck laughed. "And I thought nobody who fought for the Yankees had any imagination," he said.

CHAPTER 10

ARMSTRONG GOT UP WITH THE CRACK of dawn and walked through the quiet house to stand on the front porch. In the east, the sun was a glowing orange ball just poised over the rim of a distant range of hills. In this early morning light the world looked as if it were painted in hues of red, orange, and amber, except for the patches of deep purple where the blue veil of night still clung in the notches and draws of the hills.

Armstrong enjoyed the idea of owning everything for as far as he could see from the red hills in the east to the purple mountains in the west. He had come out here determined to carve an empire and he was well on his way to reaching that goal. He was particularly proud of the fact that everything he had accomplished so far, had been done without the gold he and the Beekman brothers had "liberated" at the end of the war.

Of course, he did let the bankers in Houston know that he had "come into some money" at the end of the war. When they suggested it might be a missing shipment of Yankee gold, he didn't confess that it was, but he didn't exactly say no. Then, he signed a note pledging the entire amount as security to back his loan. However, that loan was now paid off and from this point on, everything Sam Armstrong did, he did on his own.

In one respect, Armstrong wished he had never taken that shipment. He had closed the chapter on his war years by that act, thus assuring that he would, forever, be a wanted man. And the irony was that it was all a waste. He had proven to himself that he was quite capable of success without the gold, and he believed he had proven to Lily Montgomery, as well, that he was a man to be reckoned with.

It had been quite a shock when he first ran across her out here. There she was, Lillian Montgomery, daughter of Cephus Montgomery, the plantation owner Armstrong had worked for before the war.

If anything, Lillian was more beautiful now than she had been when she was the daughter of the wealthiest planter in northern Mississippi, and clearly, the most beautiful and desirable young lady in Itawamba County. Armstrong had been smitten by the lovely young daughter of his employer, so he went to the plantation owner and told him of his feelings for her. He asked for permission to call on her.

"Sir," Cephus Montgomery had responded. "I am flattered that you find my daughter desirable. But surely you can understand that there are certain, rather delicate, personal reasons why I would prefer that you not call on her."

Armstrong wouldn't let it go at that. He pressed the matter until finally, Montgomery had to expand on his feelings.

"Mr. Armstrong, I have tried to spare your feelings. I know that it isn't easy for you, under the circumstances. But, all delicacy aside, sir, I intend to see to it that Lillian makes a genteel marriage. A genteel marriage, sir, is one to a man, not only of property, but who can sire grandchildren I will be proud of. You are an able overseer, but you do not meet those standards. It isn't merely the question of children, nor is it a question of one's background. In fact, I admire the man who can rise above his background. You, sir, have failed to do so. You are uncouth, overly ambitious, and insensitive to what your condition will mean to my daughter, or to any woman who might marry you. I had hoped you would spare me the embarrassment of calling to your attention what you must surely already know. However, you chose to press matters and therefore

I must tell you now, as forcefully as I possibly can, that I have absolutely no intention of ever allowing you to call upon my daughter."

Angered by the strong words of his employer, Armstrong quit his position shortly after that incident. Then came the war, and Armstrong's path led him to new destinies.

Cephus Montgomery went to war as well, and was killed at Vicksburg. Shortly after her father died, Lillian's mother died of typhoid, and all the Montgomery land was confiscated for taxes.

After the death of her father and mother, and the loss of the plantation to taxes, Lillian found herself dependent upon her own resources for survival. She left Mississippi, and, after a series of misadventures, wound up in Texas, not as Lillian Montgomery, Belle of Itawamba County, but as Lily Montgomery, bordello queen.

As far as Armstrong could determine, Lily had never gone "on the line" herself, but that was of little matter. She had been the madam of a bordello before, and the Easy Pickin's Hotel and Saloon was little more than that now. That was certainly a far enough descent from the "genteel" lady her father had thought her to be.

Despite the depths to which Lily Montgomery had fallen, however, she was still a proud woman. When she was confronted by Armstrong, she held her head up, making no apologies for her position. Armstrong admired that about her. Surely, he thought, she would no longer be concerned about the proper breeding of children. Surely, now, the original objections her father had to the marriage would be gone. Armstrong was positive she would welcome his proposal now, as a means of reestablishing herself in proper society.

Armstrong was wrong. She turned him down. He was surprised and angered when she refused. She refused politely, but she did refuse.

By that time, Armstrong had already begun his plan of forcing all the other ranchers out of business so that he could own the entire range. He extended that idea to include buying up the town as well. It was his intention to get himself in such a position of power within the town that he could dictate terms to Lily. He now owned a substantial part of the town, and would have owned the Easy Pickin's as well, had Jess Langdon not given Lily the money she needed to buy back her note from the bank.

Langdon had not only prevented him from buying Lily's hotel, he had also organized the ranchers so that it was more difficult for him to run everyone else out. And Langdon had hired the two Chaney brothers.

He wondered what the Chaneys were waiting for. He knew they had come here to find him, but they had been here for six weeks now, and he had yet to meet them face-to-face. He knew that the confrontation was coming, but when? For God's sake, why didn't they just come on out here and get it over with?

Well, let them come and be damned. He would be ready for them.

Armstrong heard a sound over near the foreman's house, and he saw a young woman come out the back door and begin pumping water. She was nude from the waist up. He hadn't learned this one's name yet. The one before had been called Elsie. This one seemed a little prettier than Elsie... certainly a little cleaner.

The Beekmans had been ridiculously easy to handle. All they were interested in was enough money to keep themselves in whiskey, women, and dude clothes. They were supposed to be his partners in Gold Dust, but neither of them had an interest in bookkeeping, nor in managing a ranch the size of this one. When he told them the ranch wasn't making money, they believed him. They didn't care, as long as he supplied them with enough money to satisfy their needs. They were completely content to leave everything to him, though they did do occasional tasks for him, such as burning the Miller house last month, or the job they did last night, when they introduced infected cows into the combined herd.

Armstrong struck a match on the porch pillar and lit his cigar, then laughed.

The other ranchers were such fools, he thought. The crazy fools made it so easy for him. They combined their herds, moving every cow on the range, except his cows, into one great herd.

Shortly after that, Armstrong heard about an infected herd up in the Territories. That was when he got the idea on how to wipe out all the ranchers in one bold move. They would be forced to sell out then, and the entire range, nearly a million acres, would belong to him.

It was easy to get the infected cows. He simply wrote a letter to the rancher with the infected herd, explaining that he was a veterinarian doing research on hoof-and-mouth disease. He had them brought to him in a special railroad car, shunted the car onto the spur line which ran to his private loading pen, then, last night, had Clay and Carl Beekman put them in with the combined herd of the Greater Texas Cattle Company.

Armstrong saw a lone rider out beyond the gate. The rider was too far away from Armstrong for him to see his features, but he didn't have to see his features to know who it was. It was Shardeen.

Shardeen made Armstrong very uneasy. Where did he stay at night? He never stayed in the bunkhouse, even though it was available to him if he wanted it. Armstrong never knew where to find him, but Shardeen always seemed to be available when he needed him.

Shardeen was certainly different from Wiggins. Of course, Wiggins wasn't really that good with a gun, the way he fancied that he was. He had earned himself a local reputation mostly by bully and bluster. He had killed a man in Brenham, and another in Hempstead, and that made people frightened of him. He was worthless as a worker, but on some occasions Armstrong had been able to use him as a means of intimidating people. In the early days of Armstrong's expansion, some of the ranchers had resisted being moved off their land. Wiggins helped convince them, though he didn't have to kill anyone to do it.

Then he had gone up against Buck Chaney, and Buck had killed him.

Armstrong knew that Buck was a courageous man. He had seen him perform during the war. He had no idea Buck was that fast with a gun, though. Of course, he was certain that Buck Chaney would be no match for Shardeen, if it ever came to that.

Nobody knew exactly how many men Shardeen had killed. Some said he had killed as many as thirty...some said the figure was much, much higher. Shardeen didn't speak about it... at least, he didn't speak with words. The first moment Armstrong ever saw him though, he knew that he was looking at pure, unrestrained evil.

Armstrong didn't really know if Shardeen was fast or not, but he knew something that most men didn't understand. The speed and accuracy one has with a gun are secondary to the willingness one has to kill. Shardeen was willing to kill anyone, anytime, anywhere, without the slightest hesitation or twinge of feeling. That made him more dangerous than someone who might have twice his speed.

Armstrong was sure that Shardeen had killed the two Simpson boys. Shardeen told him that he found them already dead, but Armstrong knew, beyond a shadow of a doubt, that Shardeen had killed them.

Armstrong hadn't specifically ordered them killed, and yet, he realized that his instructions to Shardeen were such that Shardeen could have interpreted them that way. Armstrong was sorry the Simpson boys were killed. He would much have preferred the ranchers to leave the range peaceably, than to die trying to defend it. But if someone had to die, better them than him.

Shardeen turned through the gate and rode, slowly, up the drive toward the porch. Armstrong waited for him.

"Someone's comin'," Shardeen said. Armstrong didn't like Shardeen's voice. It was like a snake and it made Armstrong's hair stand on end.

"Who is it?"

"The marshal and the Chaney brothers," Shardeen said.

"The Chaneys? Here?" Armstrong said anxiously. "What are they doing here?"

"I don't know. Do you want me to kill them?"

"No!" Armstrong said quickly. "Uh, that is, not
unless they...I mean..."

"You afraid of them?" Shardeen asked.

"Yes," Armstrong admitted.'

"Why? What did you do to them?"

"It was a...a long time ago, during the war," Armstrong said.

The three riders Shardeen had mentioned
came into view now, and Armstrong ground out
his cigar as he waited for them. He had never met
Lance Chaney, but he recognized Buck at once. He
realized then that he wasn't wearing a gun, and he
started to go back in the house to get one. Then he
decided against it. It would be safer if he didn't have
a gun. Besides, Chism was with them. Armstrong
had Chism in his hip pocket. The Chaney brothers
weren't going to do anything with Chism and Shardeen both here.

"Colonel Armstrong," Buck said, as the three
men reined up in front of the house.

Armstrong stroked the scar on the side of his
face. "It's Barlow," he replied.

"Ah, yes, Barlow, of course," Buck said.

"You must be Buck Chaney."

Buck smiled. "And so I must," he said. He nodded at Lance. "My brother, Lance."

"What can I do for you gentlemen?"

"We've been looking for you for quite a while," Buck said.

"You can't have been looking too hard. I've been right here ever since you boys arrived in town and shot down my best man."

"If he was your best man, help must be hard to find," Buck said. Buck looked at Shardeen, but Shardeen was unmoving, unflinching. If Shardeen perceived Buck's remark as a barb at him, he didn't show it. In fact, he showed nothing at all. "Anyway, you know what I'm talking about. I've been looking for you ever since you took the gold."

"Gold? What gold? I don't know anything about any gold."

"Surely you remember, Colonel. We're talking about the nearly one million dollars in gold dust you stole," Lance said.

Marshal Chism gasped and looked at Buck and Lance in surprise. "What? What did you say? One million dollars in gold?"

"Why...you're crazy!" Armstrong sputtered. "I don't have any gold!" Armstrong looked over at Shardeen and saw something in the gunman's face that terrified him even more than the challenge from the Chaney brothers. Shardeen, for the first time since Armstrong had met him, exhibited an interest in something. "I admit," he went on, "that I am Armstrong. Samuel Barlow Armstrong. I came out here after the war and changed my name, but so did a lot of other people. I fought for the South in a way that wasn't too popular, so I had paper out on me. And I admit, I may have kept a dollar or two from some of the raids. But a million dollars?" Armstrong tried to laugh, but the laugh was weak and forced. "Whatever gave you such a preposterous idea?"

"I told you where I hid the money," Buck said. "You are the only one I told. That means you have it."

"We ain't got it," a new voice said, and Buck looked over to see Clay and Carl Beekman coming toward them from one of the smaller buildings. Both the Beekmans were carrying shotguns, and the shotguns were pointed toward Buck, Lance, and Marshal Chism.

"Hey, just a minute here!" Chism said. "Colonel Barlow, your men are pointing scatterguns at me!"

"Then get the hell out of the line of fire," Clay Beekman said easily. He chuckled. "It's been a long time, Cap'n."

"I might've known you two would team up with

him," Buck said. "Neither one of you have sense enough to be on your own."

"I'd be watchin' my mouth if I was you, Cap'n," Clay said. "You ain't facin' no young kid with a revolver now. Me and Carl's both holdin' scatterguns, and we know how to use them."

"I'm sure you do," Buck said. Buck looked at Armstrong and smiled. "Well, maybe you don't know anything about the gold," he said. "Maybe it was someone else."

Armstrong smiled nervously. "Sure, it could have been anyone," he said. "There were a lot of people around then, if you recall. The North and the South had groups of guerrillas riding through there all the time. I swear to you, as soon as I learned the war was over, I left the country. I had no intention of spending any time in a Union prison. Clay and Carl left with me. They can tell you."

"That's right, Cap'n," Carl said. "We'uns all left together."

Buck reached down and patted the neck of his horse. He looked at the shotguns which were held, unwaveringly, on him and his brother. He looked at the man he knew was called Shardeen, and he knew that Shardeen was instant death to anyone who might be so foolish as to challenge him.

"Uh, listen, Captain Chaney," Armstrong went on, "I know you and your brother are working for

Langdon. I don't know what he's paying you, but, well, you were a good man when you rode for me. I wouldn't mind having you ride for me again. You and your brother. And I'll double whatever it is you and your brother are getting now."

"Well, now, Colonel, my brother and I appreciate that," Buck said. "We really do. But we started down this trail with Jess, so, I reckon we'll just see it through to the end."

"You're going to lose, you know," Armstrong said. "Within six more months, I'm going to own every piece of property on this entire range."

"Maybe so," Buck said. "But then you know what a sucker I am for lost causes. After all, I did fight for the Confederacy."

"I didn't," Lance put in, coldly. "I didn't lose then, and I don't intend to lose now."

"Come on, Lance," Buck said. "I guess we'd better be getting back." Buck pulled his horse around, then, almost as an afterthought, he stooped and looked back at Armstrong. "Oh, by the way, I almost forgot the reason we came out here this morning."

"I wondered when you would get around to that," Armstrong said. He pulled out a cigar and lit it. "You've been here for six weeks, but this is the first time you've come out to see me. What made you decide to come now?"

"You tell him, big brother."

Lance smiled, coldly. "Just a neighborly gesture on our part, that's all," he said. He leaned forward and patted the neck of his mount. "It seems that last night a couple of your cows almost wandered into our herd. Fortunately, we saw them before they got mixed up with our cows, or we may not have been able to pick them out. Anyway, we brought them back."

"What?" Armstrong gasped.

"We put them in the pen with that herd of blood-ed Herefords you are so proud of," Buck added. "You can't miss them. As a matter of fact, they are sort of sickly looking, if you ask me."

"No!" Armstrong choked. He looked at the Beek-mans. "Don't just stand there, you dumb bastards! Go find those two cows and kill them!"

"Kill them?" Chism asked, confused by Armstrong's reaction. "Colonel Barlow, why do you want to kill them?"

"It's Armstrong, you stupid son of a bitch!" Armstrong growled. "And I want to kill them because they have hoof-and-mouth disease. Don't you understand? If those cows infect my herd, I'll be ruined. Ruined!"

"Really?" Lance said easily. "Then I guess it's a lucky break for the ranchers that we saw the cows before they got into the combined herd, isn't it?"

"You dumb bastards!" Armstrong shouted at

Clay and Carl. "You are responsible for this! You!"

"Hey, what are you mad at us for?" Clay asked. "We just did what you told us to do."

"Get the hell out there!" Armstrong ordered. "Get out there and find them! Find those cows! Find them before it is too late."

"Oh, I think it's already too late," Buck said easily. "It only takes five minutes for a sick cow to infect a well cow, and five minutes for that cow to infect another, and then another…why, by now half your herd is probably infected and rubbing up against the other half. I'm sorry, Armstrong…I don't think there's anything you can do about it now. Come along, Marshal. We'd better report this. I suspect the Texas Cattlemen's Association will want to make certain the entire Gold Dust herd is destroyed before this disease spreads any farther."

"I'll get you for this, Buck Chaney!" Armstrong shouted as Buck, Lance, and Chism rode away. "I'll get you for this!"

CHAPTER 11

ARMSTRONG KILLED TEN OF HIS FINEST Herefords before he discovered that he had been tricked. The two cows the Chaneys had introduced to his herd didn't have hoof-and-mouth disease. In fact, they weren't even the same two cows the Beekmans had taken over to the combined herd. When he discovered the ruse he grew angry with the Beekmans, because he knew it was their incompetence which had caused it. If they had done their job correctly the two cows wouldn't have been discovered until it was too late.

"Wait a minute," Clay said. "You're the one wanted to put the sick cows in with the herd. That wasn't our idea."

"There was nothing wrong with the idea, you dumb bastards," Armstrong replied. "The idea was a good one. I just hadn't counted on you two being so dumb that you couldn't do it."

"Who are you callin' dumb?" Carl asked.

"I'm calling you dumb," Armstrong said. "You and that stupid brother of yours. In fact, I've had about all I can stomach of the two of you, and I want you to get out of here. Get out, now. Get off my ranch."

"You can't kick us off this here ranch, Armstrong," Clay said. "This ain't your ranch alone, this here ranch belongs to me and my brother, just as much as it belongs to you."

Armstrong smiled at them. "Do you really think I would be so dumb as to let your names appear on any deeds of property or water rights? Gold Dust, and everything on it, belongs to me and me alone. As far as I'm concerned you two have never been anything but hands...and not very good hands at that. Now I'm ordering you off my property."

"We ain't goin'."

"Shardeen," Armstrong said quietly.

Shardeen took one step toward the Beekman brothers and both of them began backing away, holding their hands out toward him.

"All right, all right," Carl said. "We're goin', we're goin'."

"But we want our share," Clay said to Armstrong. "You hear me, Armstrong? We want our share!"

"You want your share of what?"

"You know of what," Clay said. "The gold. We want our share of the gold."

Armstrong laughed. "You fools. Do you really think there's any of that left? It's taken every bit of that, and then some, to build what I have here. Believe me, there's no gold left. None."

"I don't believe you."

"It doesn't matter whether you believe me or not," Armstrong said. "You are leaving."

"You ain't shootin' straight with us, Armstrong," Carl said. "Maybe you did spend all the gold, but you got this ranch. What do we get out of all this?"

"If you leave now, gentlemen, you may leave with your lives," Armstrong offered.

The Beekmans looked toward Shardeen once more, then Clay spoke.

"Come on, Carl," he said. "Let's go."

It took them no more than five minutes to pack their belongings and saddle their horses. The girl who had been staying with them realized that her meal ticket was about to end. As they were climbing on their horses, she ran out to them, carrying her own clothes tied up in a bundle.

"What about me, honey?" she asked. "You are going to take me with you, aren't you? You aren't going to leave me here?"

Clay had already mounted his horse and she was pulling on his leg as she pleaded with him. Clay kicked at her, much as he would at a dog.

"Get the hell out of here," he growled. "Come on, Carl, let's ride."

Carl and Clay dug their spurs into their horses and the animals broke into a gallop, throwing sand and gravel as they rode away.

The Beekmans were not at all liked by the other hands on the place. They never worked, yet they were obviously the highest paid hands around. No one quite understood the relationship between the man they called Colonel Barlow, and the two brothers. They still didn't fully understand why he had kept them around for as long as he had, but they knew now that the brothers were being fired and that was good enough for them. They began laughing and hooting and they chased the Beekmans off with their catcalls.

"Don't you worry none about the girl, boys," one of the hands called to them. "We'll take care of her. We'll take care of her real good!"

The Beekmans rode hard for ten minutes, then when they were about three miles away from the main house, they stopped their horses to give them a blow.

"That son of a bitch!" Clay swore. "He stole it from us, Carl! The son of a bitch stole our gold!"

"We should've killed him," Carl answered. "We shouldn't have left like that. We should have stood up to the bastard and killed him."

"With Shardeen there, we wouldn't have even cleared leather," Clay said.

"I don't care," Carl said. "It just galls me that we left like whipped dogs."

"Our time will come," Clay said. "You remember Deekus? We finally got him, didn't we?"

"Yeah," Carl said. He chuckled. "He never knew what hit him."

"No one did," Clay said. "Not even Armstrong. Everyone thought it was just a lucky Yankee bullet got Deekus, but it was us."

"We sure got away with that clean," Carl said. "It makes me feel good to know that son of a bitch is dead."

"Yeah," Clay said. "Well, you're goin' to feel that way about Armstrong pretty soon, too, because the Chaneys are goin' to take care of him for us. You think they goin' to just stand by and do nothin' about their sister?"

Carl laughed. "I guess you're right at that. You know, the funniest thing is…Armstrong's goin' to get himself killed for that, and he don't even know nothin' about it."

Clay rubbed his crotch. "She was fine, brother. Oh, she was so fine," he said.

"Yeah. Too bad you had to kill her."

"I didn't have no choice. She was goin' to scream. Still, she was fine."

"Well, let's get goin'," Carl said. "Not much future in stayin' around here anymore."

Suddenly, from the other side of the ridgeline which ran parallel to the course they had ridden, Shardeen appeared in front of them.

"Shardeen!" Clay gasped.

"Hold it!" Shardeen hissed, and he held his hand out toward them. "I didn't come to kill you!"

"What...what did you come for?" Carl asked.

"I came to make a deal," Shardeen answered.

"A deal? What kind of a deal?"

"I know where the gold is," Shardeen said.

"What? How could you? You didn't even know about the gold until the Chaneys mentioned it."

"I know," Shardeen hissed. "But as soon as Chaney mentioned gold, then I knew where it had to be. I figured Barlow was keeping somethin' valuable there and I figured I'd have a look-see someday. Now that I know what it is, I'm ready for that day to be soon."

"Why...why are you tellin' us?" Clay wanted to know.

"Is it true? Did you really take one million dollars in gold?"

"Nine hundred thousand," Clay said.

"And you seen it?"

"Seen it? Hell, we lugged it near a thousand miles," Clay said.

"Damn near four-hundred pounds of it," Carl added.

"That's a lot of gold," Shardeen said. "Too much gold for one man to carry off by himself. I need help."

"You're right about that," Clay said. "So, you figure on cuttin' yourself in for a share, do you?"

"Half."

"Half? But there are two of us. It should be by thirds," Carl said.

"Half for me, half for the two of you," Shardeen said.

"But that ain't right," Carl protested. "It's rightly our gold in the first place."

"You don't like it, I'll get someone else to help me."

Clay sighed. "We got no choice, Carl. We either go along with him, or we're out of it."

"All right," Carl agreed. "Half it is. Now, where is he keeping it?"

"The north fireplace in the parlor don't draw," Shardeen said.

"What?" Carl asked. "It don't draw? What the hell is that supposed to mean."

"It means it's a fake chimney," Clay said. "Yes, that's it. He's built a vault into that fireplace."

"All right, so if it is, how do we get it out?" Carl asked. "I mean, we can't just go get it in broad daylight."

"And I ain't about to go messin' around there at night," Clay added.

"I'll take care of that," Shardeen promised. "Tomorrow mornin', I'll have everyone off the ranch."

"Everyone?"

"Yes."

"How are you goin' to do that?"

"Just leave it to me," Shardeen said. "When they're gone, you two get the gold and meet me in Rattlesnake Canyon. We'll divide it there."

"All right," Carl said. "We'll do it."

"Good." Shardeen started to ride away, but Clay called out to him.

"Shardeen?"

Shardeen stopped and looked back at him.

"What makes you think we won't just take the gold and run with it?"

"Because I don't think you're ready to die," Shardeen answered easily.

"All right, then I have another question. What's to keep you from killin' us and takin' it all once we get it for you?"

"Nothin'," Shardeen hissed. He turned his horse then, and rode back toward the main house without so much as another word. Carl and Clay watched him ride away for a few moments.

"What will keep him from killin' us, Clay?"

"Simple," Clay said. "He's goin' to meet us in Rat-tlesnake Canyon, right?"

"Yeah."

"We'll be there first, waitin' for him. As soon as we see him, we'll ambush him."

Carl smiled. "Yeah," he said. "Yeah, I like that idea. I like it a lot."

"Come on," Clay suggested. "Let's get someplace where we can watch the ranch. I want to be ready to move as soon as Shardeen gets everyone away."

The next morning, in the town of Barlow, Lily got out of bed and walked over to her second-story window to look down onto the street. It was soft and quiet under the early morning light. She saw two heavily loaded freight wagons moving slowly down the street. The drivers were sitting on the seats holding the reins, already tired from the long day's haul they had in front of them. They drove their wagons past the railroad locomotive which was sitting on the turnaround loop, cold and with-out steam. The fact that they were going to take all day to carry a load to Brenham which could have been taken by the train in less than an hour, was mute, but powerful evidence of the effectiveness of the boycott the ranchers were making against Arm-strong. Indeed, the train only made one round-trip daily now, and it was just for passengers and mail. Except for Armstrong's personal use, the freight operation had been completely shut down.

By now word was all over town about the business with the infected cattle. Everyone knew that Barlow, whom they were now calling Armstrong, had tried to introduce diseased cattle into the combined herd. As far as they were concerned, the fact that he began shooting his own animals when he thought the diseased cows were returned, was proof of his guilt. There were some who felt sorry for the cows which were needlessly destroyed, but no one felt sorry for Armstrong. In fact, they all thought it was a tremendous joke on him, and last night there were several rounds drunk to the event.

Jess Langdon had celebrated a little too much and decided to spend the night in the hotel, sending the Chaneys on out to his ranch to make certain everything was all right. The Chaney brothers, strangers just over a month ago, were now accorded the status of top hands.

Lily thought of the Chaney brothers, and what a tremendous change had been brought about by their arrival. Until they came along, the ranchers were being swallowed up, one by one. And though the idea of uniting the herds was conceived by Jess Langdon and Emerson Gray, she knew that without the Chaneys, the idea would never have succeeded.

Lily knew that Buck was seeing a lot of Lucinda Gray. Lily liked Lucinda, though their social positions kept them separated. Lily had a saloon to run, while Lucinda was safe and secure on the ranch of a father and mother who loved her. Of course, Lucinda could entertain girlish dreams of romance and marriage. Had the war not come along, Lily might very well have reached that same stage of life.

But the war did come along, and the life Lily once knew was destroyed. She had been forced not only to grow up fast, but to grow up in a hostile world. The rose-colored glasses through which Lucinda looked at life, had been cruelly removed from Lily's eyes, and Lily found that she could see things more clearly as a result.

For example, there was something Lily had never told anyone, nor even admitted to herself. Lily could very easily fall in love with Lance Chaney. She could have the same intense feelings about Lance that Lucinda had about Buck. She also knew the futility of it... and that was her advantage over Lucinda. Lucinda was committing her heart to Buck Chaney and Buck, like Lance, was not the kind of man a woman should fall in love with. Buck and Lance were both driven by some demon. She didn't know what it was...but she knew that it was powerful and all- consuming, and neither she nor Lucinda would be able to breach the walls the demon had built around the Chaney brothers' hearts.

Lily sighed. There was not only no place in her life for such romantic ambitions, there wasn't even such a place for her thoughts. She turned away from the window and went into the bathroom which opened off her bedroom. She had a genuine porcelain bathtub in that room, and running water from a tank which was located on the roof of the building. It was the one luxury she allowed herself, and as she drew the water and watched the bubbles form from her bubble bath, she smiled. Maybe this wasn't the life she had planned for herself, but she was content with it.

Lily spent over half an- hour just soaking in the tub, and would have stayed longer, had she not heard the shouts. At first it was just a man's voice, muffled and indistinct, but it was joined by another, and then another. Soon she realized there were several people down on the street in front of the hotel and they were obviously agitated about something. Curious, she stepped out of the tub and slipped into a bathrobe, then she walked back to the window to look outside.

What greeted her when she looked out the window was a crowd of more than two-dozen angry men. They were shouting at each other and some of them were waving guns. A horse moved down the street at a gallop, its rider yelling at people who were looking out from buildings.

Lily stepped out onto the balcony and up to the railing. She saw Jess Langdon and Marshal Chism standing down in the middle of the crowd.

"Jess? What is it? What's wrong?" she called down.

"It's Caldwell and Oliver, Miss Lily," Langdon shouted up to her. "You know them, the freight drivers?"

"Yes, of course I know them. What about them? I just saw them."

"You just saw them? Where? When?" Marshal Chism asked.

"Why, down there on the street a short while ago," Lily answered. "I saw them as they were leaving with their loads."

"Well, they didn't get very far," Langdon said. He pointed across the street and Lily saw one of the two freight wagons parked in front of the general store. She also saw two bodies stretched out in back of the wagon.

"My God! What happened?"

"They was shot," one of the other men said. "Both of 'em."

"Armstrong did it," another said.

"Now hold on there," Chism said. "We don't know that Armstrong did this."

"The hell we don't. You know how he felt about their freight line. You know it was takin' business away from his railroad."

"That don't prove he shot them."

"It's all the proof I need," one of the men answered. "You're the law around here, Chism. Go get them."

"Now hold on, just you hold on," Chism said. "Let's don't go rushin' into things."

"You're scared to go get him. Why don't you admit it?"

"Maybe I am," Chism admitted. "Suppose I make you a deputy. You want to go get Armstrong?"

"He's got you there, Pete."

"Well, what the hell?" Pete asked angrily. "How long are we goin' to let this stuff just go on? First he dammed up all the creeks and streams, then he burned Miller's house."

"We got no proof he burned Miller's house," Chism said quickly.

"You know damn well he done it," Pete replied. "And he killed the Simpson boys, too. And now this."

"Pete's right about one thing, Chism," one of the other men said. "We can't just let this go on forever. We got to make a stand somewhere. Now it's time for the nut-cuttin'. Are you against us, or for us?"

"Suppose I ride out there and ask him to come in and talk about it?" Chism replied.

"Ask him? Ha! And when he says, 'No, thank you, I don't care to come into town just now,' what will you do?"

"I don't know," Chism admitted, defeated by the problem. He sighed. "I just don't know."

"Look! Look, there's that gunman he hired. There's Shardeen!"

Lily looked down at the opposite end of the street toward the object of everyone's attention. She saw a tall, gaunt man sitting on his horse with his leg cocked casually across the pommel. It was obvious he had been watching the crowd for several minutes and now that they saw him, he sat up straight and urged his horse toward them. The hollow clopping of the animal's hooves sounded unusually loud as everyone had stopped all conversation and activity to watch him approach.

"Shardeen," Chism said, when Shardeen drew near. "Shardeen, do you know anything about what happened to Caldwell and Oliver?"

Shardeen looked over toward the wagon.

"They're dead," he said easily.

"Yes, they are," Langdon said. "And I want to know if you know anything about it?"

"No," Shardeen said. "I don't know anything about it."

"You're a liar!" someone shouted. Shardeen looked toward the crowd with his cold snake eyes, but he showed no emotion over the insult, nor did he even try to determine who said it. Everyone in the crowd drew back from his gaze.

"What are you doing in town, Shardeen?" Langdon asked. "Why are you here?"

"I came to deliver a message," Shardeen replied.

"A message? What message?"

"Tell the ranchers and the townies who support the ranchers, that Colonel Armstrong and all of his men are coming into town this afternoon to settle accounts."

"To settle accounts. What...what are you talking about?"

"I think you know," Shardeen said. "We're taking over."

"What? Why...this is crazy! You can't do this! You can't just bully an entire town into submission!" Shardeen turned and started to ride away. "Abner," Langdon ordered. "You'd better get a telegraph off to the county sheriff. Tell him to get us some help down here, quick."

Shardeen stopped and looked back at the group of men. "Save your energy," he said. "I cut the telegraph wire. You're on your own."

It took Shardeen half-an-hour to reach the front gate of Gold Dust. There were three hands there, working on the fence. They looked up as Shardeen rode through the gate.

One of the cowboys was rolling a cigarette and he spoke. "Howdy, Shardeen. Where you been?"

"I'll bet he's been beddin' one of the girls over at

the Easy Pickin's," one of the other hands said. "I know that's where I'd be if I had any money."

Shardeen got down from his horse and walked toward them.

The man with the rail held it up to the post and his friend started to nail it up. "Now, don't tell me you're goin' to help us with this fence," the one with the hammer said. "That'll be the day."

Shardeen pulled his pistol and pointed it at them. "Hey, what the hell is this? What are you doin'? Listen, this ain't very funny!"

Shardeen squeezed off three quick shots, and all three of the men grabbed their chest as blood spilled through their fingers. The one with the rolled, but unlit cigarette fell back onto the fence. The other two pitched forward. Shardeen shot each one of them a second time, though it was unnecessary for two of them. He reached down and took the cigarette from the fingers of one of the dead cowboys and lit it, then began loading their bodies into the wagon. He was going to take them to Armstrong.

CHAPTER 12

THE THREE MEN'S NAMES WERE CURLY, Hank, and Billy. They had last names of course, but no one who worked at Gold Dust knew them. That was fairly common among the cowboys who drifted from ranch to ranch, town to town, and sometimes from as far away as Kansas or Colorado. There was a saying among the cowboys that excess names, like excess baggage, tended to slow a person down.

Someone said he thought Curly had a sister somewhere, but they had no idea where she was, or how to get hold of her so they decided to take care of their own. The three were laid out on the front porch of the foreman's house...the house that was once occupied by the Beekman brothers, but was now empty. Somehow they looked much smaller in death than they had while they were alive and the ranch hands filed by quietly and looked at them.

"It's a damn shame," one of them said. "None of them three boys ever hurt a livin' soul."

"Why, Curly would give you the shirt off his back."

"And sing... I ain't never heard nobody could sing like Billy."

"Hank could read and write, did you know that? He once wrote a letter for me."

"Who do you know to write a letter to?"

"It weren't to no one. It was to a mail-order catalogue. You know that-there sheepskin coat I got. If it weren't for old Hank writin' that letter for me, why, I never would've got it."

As the hands talked, the attributes of the three dead cowboys grew and grew and their own bitterness increased until the blood of all of them was boiling for revenge.

"Who would do a low-down skunk deed like this, anyhow?" one of the men wanted to know.

"I recognized the Chaneys," Shardeen said. "And Gray, Langdon, Miller, and Simpson. There was about a dozen of the other ranchers and quite a few from town."

"You couldn't stop them?" Armstrong asked. He had been totally shocked when Shardeen drove the wagon in with his own horse tied to the rear, and with the three bodies in the back.

"I told you," Shardeen said. "I was a long ways

off. I heard the shots, but by the time I got there, the Chaneys and the others were already headed back for town, out of range. I figured I'd bring the bodies on back here and tell you what happened."

"Yes," Armstrong said. He rubbed his scar. "Yes, you did the right thing."

"Colonel, what are we goin' to do about this?" one of the cowboys asked.

"Yeah," one of the others said. "We ain't just goin' to let them get away with it, are we?"

"What do you want to do about it?" Armstrong asked.

"By God, I'll tell you what I want to do," one of the men said. "I want to go to town and clean that place out. We ain't never goin' to have peace around here until that bunch of troublemakers is run out anyway. Hell, I say let's just go ahead and do it. Do it and be damned."

"Come on, Colonel. What do you say? We ain't goin' to let them get away with this, are we?"

"This is your chance to finish it," Shardeen hissed. "If you get things settled today, you'll control the entire range, just like you been wantin'."

"Yes," Armstrong agreed. He sighed. "I didn't want it to come to this, but I guess I have no choice now. All right," he said to his men. "I say we go to town and take care of this once and for all. Now, who is going to ride with me?"

"Yahoo!" someone shouted, and his yell was echoed by everyone present.

"Then go get your guns," Armstrong shouted. "Get your guns and get mounted up. We're going into town!"

The men whistled and cheered at the announcement, so thrilled by the excitement of what lay before them that all thoughts of sorrow over the untimely death of three of their own was put aside.

Buck, Lance, and Jess Langdon were standing at the livery stable which was on the edge of town nearest Armstrong's ranch. Emerson Gray, Miller, and Simpson were back down in the town, organizing the others in defense of the town. If Armstrong, Shardeen, and the Gold Dust hands really were coming in, they would be coming this way. They had been there for fifteen minutes or so, when Buck decided he would climb to the roof to see if he could spot them any earlier.

"Be careful you don't fall and break your fool neck," Lance said. "It'd be about like you to do something like that now."

"Don't you worry about me, big brother," Buck replied. "I'd soak my pants in coal oil and kick the devil in the ass for a chance at Armstrong. I'm not going to do anything that would let this chance get away from me."

Buck grabbed a crossbeam then started climbing. Within a moment he was on the roof, then he crawled on up to the peak.

"Can you see any better?" Lance asked.

"Yeah, a little," Buck called down. "Still don't see anything though."

Jess and Lance were left alone on the ground. "So," Jess said after a moment of silence. "It's coming down to it now. I guess after today it'll all be over, one way or another."

"Buck and I have waited for this moment for a long time," Lance said. He turned the cylinder of his revolver slowly, checking to make certain each chamber had a load.

Jess looked at him and measured his intensity. There was more to it than this showdown, and he wanted to know what it was.

"Lance, what is it? Why are you and Buck after Armstrong? Don't get me wrong, I'm glad you are, it puts you on our side and in my way of lookin' at things, that puts you on the side of right. But I am curious."

"Her name was Becky," Lance said quietly.

"Who?"

"Our sister," Lance went on. "She was eighteen years old. Only eighteen." Lance looked out into the direction from which they expected Armstrong, and a blood vessel in his temple worked.

"What about your sister?" Jess asked.

"Armstrong killed her," Lance said.

"In a guerrilla raid?"

Lance looked at Jess and shook his head slowly. "No," he said. "No guerrilla raid. The war was over when this happened. The war was already over when he raped her...and when he killed her."

"My God! He raped her?"

"Yes," Lance said.

"It's no wonder you've been chasing him so long. The wonder is that you didn't kill him when you first got here."

"It wouldn't have done us any good to kill him, then face a murder charge," Lance said. "We've had a year for the rage to cool down. That gave us the luxury of planning it. Believe me, once we found him, we weren't going to let him get away. It was just a matter of finding the right time, that's all."

"Well, I guess you've done that. It looks to me like that time is now."

"Here they come!" Buck called down from the peak of the roof. He turned around and slid down to the eave, then dropped down to the ground. "They are about a mile away."

"I'll signal the others," Jess said. He stepped out onto the street and held his rifle up over his head. All up and down the street men found positions of cover and concealment. Gray and the others had done their job well, for Lance could see them lying behind the corner of porches, behind water troughs, inside doors and windows, on the roofs, and behind the false fronts of the buildings.

"Looks like he's riding into a hornets' nest," Lance said.

"Yeah," Buck replied. "And that's what's bothering me."

"What do you mean?"

"I knew this son of a bitch in the war, remember? He wasn't one to make a frontal assault then, and I don't think he is now. I just can't believe that he's going to come right in. He's going to pull something."

"Let him try any trick he wants," Lance said. "He's not getting away from us."

"Buck? Lance?" Jess said. Jess had been looking toward the approaching riders while Lance and Buck were surveying the town's defenses. "They're stopping. There's just two riders coming in alone."

"Maybe they want to parley," Buck suggested. He looked toward the approaching riders. "Look's like Armstrong is holding up a white flag."

"All right," Langdon said. "We'll let them come in...see what they have to say."

"You'd better yell at the others," Lance suggested. "Make sure no one gets an itchy trigger finger."

"Yeah, I guess you're right," Jess said. "Caldwell

and Oliver had a lot of friends in town...some of them might be looking for a little revenge." He started down the street, waving his arms. "Hold your fire!" he shouted. "Hold your fire! We're going to parley!"

Buck and Lance stepped out into the street as the two riders entered town.

"You've got a lot of nerve coming into town like this, Armstrong," Buck said. "More nerve than I remember you for."

"I want a meeting," Armstrong replied. "In the Easy Pickin's Saloon."

"Do you now?"

"I want Gray, Langdon, and you two down at the saloon. We'll be waiting for you down there."

"Armstrong, seems to me like you aren't in any position to demand much of anything," Buck said.

Armstrong twisted around in his saddle and pointed to his men who were waiting about two hundred yards beyond the edge of town.

"We can talk or we can fight," Armstrong said. "If we fight in town a lot of people are going to be killed. Some of them may be women and kids."

"He's got a point there, Lance," Buck suggested. Lance stroked his chin for a moment. "All right," he said. "You go on down to the saloon. We'll get Gray and Langdon and meet you there."

Armstrong smiled. "I thought you might see

things my way." He clucked at his horse and he and Shardeen rode down to the saloon while Buck and Lance collected the others for the meeting.

Fred, Lily, and Ann were inside the saloon. When Fred saw Armstrong and Shardeen come through the batwing doors, he started toward the back of the bar where he kept his scattergun. Shardeen pointed his pistol toward him.

"Miss," Shardeen hissed to Lily. "If you want your barkeep alive, you'd better tell him to sit down at the table here, with the two of you."

"Fred," Lily said. "Do what he says!"

Fred moved away from the bar and sat at the table with Lily and Ann.

"That's more like it," Shardeen said.

"Miss Lily, what is it? What's going on?" Ann asked in a frightened tone. Because Ann had "worked" the night before, she slept in this morning. She had no idea that there was a battle brewing between the town and Gold Dust.

"Mr. Armstrong had Caldwell and Oliver killed this morning," Lily said. "I guess now he thinks it's time for a showdown."

Armstrong looked over toward Lily with a surprised expression on his face. "Caldwell and Oliver? The freight drivers?"

"Yes, the freight drivers, as you well know," Lily spat at him.

"Why do you say I had them killed? I don't know anything about that."

"They're lying over in the hardware store right now, waiting for coffins to be built," Lily said.

"I told you, I don't know anything about that. What I do know is that a bunch of men from this so-called 'Cattle Company' killed three of my men this morning. They rode out there and shot them down in cold blood."

"Who did?" Lily asked.

"Your friend Langdon for one. And the Chaneys and Emerson Gray."

"This morning, you say?"

"Yes."

"That's not true," Lily said. "At least, not for Jess Langdon. I know for a fact that he spent the night in town and he's been here all morning long."

"You say he didn't do it, but I've got three dead cowboys on my hands. And I'm saying I don't know anything about a couple of dead freight drivers, but you tell me they're lying over in the hardware store. Maybe it's a good thing we're having this meeting. It's about time we started getting things straightened out around here, once and for all."

Shardeen looked at the Regulator clock on the wall. "I reckon I can clear some of it up," he said. "By now the Beekmans have done their job."

"The Beekmans? I fired the Beekmans."

"I rehired them."

"Who are you to hire them?"

"I'm the one who is running things around here now," Shardeen said. He looked over at Lily. "The freight drivers? I killed them."

"What?" Armstrong said. "Why, man? Why did you kill them? They didn't have anything to do with killing Curly, Hank, and Billy."

"I know they didn't," Shardeen said easily. "I killed them, too."

"You what?"

Shardeen pointed his pistol at Armstrong and pulled the hammer back. The cylinder clicked into place.

"Shardeen, what are you doing?" Armstrong gasped. "Why are you doing this?"

"To get the gold," Shardeen said. "I set all this up to get everyone away from the ranch. While everyone was gone this morning, the Beekmans got the gold. The fools think they are going to share with me."

"No, you are the one who is the fool!" Armstrong said. "You don't know what you are doing. There—"

Armstrong wasn't able to finish his statement because Shardeen shot him. The bullet knocked Armstrong back against the bar. He threw his arm out to try and hold himself up, knocked over a bottle of whiskey, then slid down to the floor. He sat there, leaning against the bar, looking out at the others with eyes which were full of pain and confusion.

The batwing doors of the saloon were pushed open then, and Buck, Lance, and the others rushed inside. Shardeen turned his gun toward them.

"Lay your guns on the table, gents," he hissed. He turned his pistol toward Lily and cocked it. The cylinder rotated with a deadly click. "Do it now, if you don't want this woman killed."

Buck put his gun down and the others followed suit. Shardeen backed through the door. Buck and Lance moved to the door and watched him as he got on his horse, then started out of town.

"Who shot Armstrong?" Buck asked, turning around.

"Shardeen shot him," Fred answered.

"What's going on here?" Lance growled. "Why did Shardeen shoot Armstrong?"

"I guess there is no honor among thieves after all," Langdon said.

Lily was on the floor beside Armstrong now, and she had positioned him so that his head was in her lap. When Buck came over to stand above him, Armstrong looked up.

"So," he said. "You have followed me this long and this far for the gold." He tried to laugh, but the laugh turned into a cough which sprayed flecks of blood on the front of his shirt. "That's funny," he said.

"What's funny?"

"That the two of you would chase me this far . . . that the Beekmans and Shardeen would betray me, all for something that doesn't exist."

"Doesn't exist? What do you mean, doesn't exist?"

"There is no gold," Armstrong said.

"You mean it's gone? You've spent it?"

"I mean I never had it," he said. "It never existed."

"Who do you think you are telling this to?" Buck demanded. "I know it existed. I held it in my hand, I buried it under the floor of my barn, remember? Nine hundred thousand dollars' worth of gold dust."

"No," Armstrong insisted. "There was just enough gold to make it look real. Gold dust, mixed with pyrite. You do know what that is, don't you?" He laughed again, and again he sprayed blood from his destroyed lungs. "Fool's gold, Captain. Fool's gold. Hell, some of the bags didn't even pretend to be gold. When I opened them I found nothing but lead…lead to make the weight. I doubt if there was nine hundred dollars' worth of gold, let alone nine hundred thousand dollars."

"Why would the Beekmans want to steal that?"

"The Beekmans were like you. They never actually looked," Armstrong said. "And I found it expedient not to let them know. You see, I discovered that if people think you're rich, it is almost as good as being rich. When the bankers thought I had nine hundred thousand dollars in gold dust, they were more than willing to make me all the loans I wanted."

"You're lying, Armstrong," Buck said. "Why would the Yankees ship a load of lead and fool's gold?"

"For a diversion," Lance said. It was the first time he had spoken since Armstrong began weaving his bizarre tale.

Buck looked around at his brother. "A diversion?"

"Yes, a diversion," Lance said bitterly. "I can see it now. Armstrong is right. That's why General Wilson was so willing for us to let it go. That's why he never really said much to me about losing it. I was supposed to lose it, little brother. I was set up. We were both set up."

"General Wilson and General Price must have gotten a big laugh out of us after we left them that night," Buck said. "The bastards!"

"And so you've come after me for nothing," Armstrong said.

"Nothing?" Buck said sharply, turning back to the wounded man. "You son of a bitch! Do you think we chased you this far just because of the gold? It was Becky that brought us after you, you bastard. Becky! The only thing I regret is that Shardeen shot you first."

"Who is Becky?"

"She's the girl you raped when you took the gold... or what you thought was the gold from our farm," Buck said. He pointed his pistol at Armstrong's face and cocked it. "Don't die on me, you son of a bitch! I don't want you to die. I want you to live, just long enough for me to kill you!"

"Captain Chaney, I swear to you, I didn't harm that girl. The last time I saw her she was ..." Armstrong paused in midsentence. "The Beekmans," he said. "They went back. They said it was to cover our trail. That must have been when it happened. I'm sorry, I didn't know anything about that. I swear I didn't."

"You expect me to believe you?"

"What do I have to gain by lying?" Armstrong asked. He coughed up more blood. "I'm shot through the lungs, Captain. We both saw enough of these wounds during the war to know what that means. I've got a few moments left, no more."

"I don't believe you," Buck said in frustrated rage. "Damnit, I can't believe you! I've chased you too far for it to end like this!"

"Lillian," Armstrong said. He gasped hard for breath. "Lillian, tell them. I know you have laughed about it enough. Tell them."

"I've never laughed about it, Sam. I swear, I've never laughed," Lily said.

"Tell them," Armstrong gasped. His breathing was coming with great difficulty now,

Lily looked up at Buck and Lance. Inexplicably, she was crying!

"Lily! Lily, what...what is this? Are you feeling sorry for this son of a bitch? Why are you crying for him? Didn't you hear what I said? He raped our sister!"

"No, he didn't," Lily said.

"What? How can you say that? How can you believe him?"

"Sam could never rape anybody. Years ago, when he was working on my father's plantation, he had an accident...a terrible accident. He isn't...he isn't whole," she said.

"The Beekmans," Armstrong said weakly. "It was the Beekmans." Armstrong's head fell to one side.

"Sam!" Lily called. "Sam!" She closed her eyes then, as tears rolled slowly down her cheeks.

At that moment Miller burst in through the swinging doors.

"That gunman's got Lucinda!" he said.

"What?" Buck asked, looking up toward him. "Some of the men decided they weren't goin' to let Shardeen get out of town," Miller said. "They took a couple of shots at him as he was leavin'. One of the shots killed his horse. That all happened just as Lucinda was comin' into town, so he grabbed her. He's holdin' her now."

"Oh, my God, I've got to get her away from that madman," Gray said, starting toward the door.

"Hold on, Mr. Gray," Buck called out to him. "You go running out there like that and you'll get yourself and Lucinda killed."

"I've got to do something!" Gray said. "I can't just stand around while that bastard has my little girl."

"You said he's holding her now," Buck asked Miller. "Where?"

"He took her into the Malone house. You know the house, don't you? It's that big two-story brick, at the edge of town."

"Yeah, I know it," Buck said. "I thought it was empty."

"It is," Langdon said. "When Doc Malone died, his widow went back to New Orleans. It's been empty for more than a year now."

Buck pulled his gun and checked the loads, then slipped it back into his holster. "All right, I'm going after her."

"I'm coming with you," Lance said.

"No," Buck said. "Get out there in the street where he can see you. Make a big thing about trying to deal with him. I need a diversion." He smiled, dryly. "You do know about diversions, don't you?" he teased. Lance smiled back. "I reckon I do at that," he said, "Jess, you and me had better go out and tell Armstrong's hands what all is going on," Miller suggested.

"Yeah, you're right."

"Oh, Jess, won't that be dangerous?" Lily asked.

"I doubt it," Jess answered. "Most of his hands are pretty good boys. They went to work out there because there was no place left to go. I don't reckon they're all that anxious to make a war, especially now that Armstrong's dead."

"I think you're right," Buck said. "And even that will help keep Shardeen's mind busy. Now tell me, is there a way I can approach the house without being seen?"

"Well, there's a gully out back of the saloon here," Fred, the barkeep, suggested. "It runs for about three- quarters of the length of the town, but it stops behind the barbershop."

"Yeah, and it's a good hundred-and-fifty feet of open ground from the barbershop to the Malone house," Langdon pointed out.

"I'll just have to figure out how to cover that last hundred-and-fifty feet when I get there," Buck said. "Get out there in the street, Lance. Get him to talk to you."

"Wait a minute," Fred said to Buck. "Mr. Chaney, let me put on your hat and shirt and I'll go out in the street with your brother. From the other end of town, he might mistake me for you."

Buck smiled. "That's a good idea," he agreed. "But he might shoot you, too."

"I just come through four years of people tryin' to shoot me," he said. "I reckon I can handle it one more time."

Buck changed shirts with Fred, then gave him his hat. When they were ready, he nodded at Lance, then Lance and the others went out the front door. Buck slipped out the back, then ran, bent over at the waist, until he reached the gully. He jumped down into it.

The gully was full of rusting tin cans, bottles, buzzing flies, and reeking garbage. Buck pulled his pistol, then started toward the west end of town in the direction of the Malone house.

"Shardeen!" Lance called from the middle of the street. "Shardeen! Langdon has gone to see all the Gold Dust hands to tell them what happened. You're all alone now."

"I ain't quite alone," Shardeen called back. "Don't forget, I got the girl with me."

"Let her go!"

There was a flash of light from one of the top windows of the house. The sound of the shot and the zing of the bullet reached Lance's ear at about the same time. The bullet hit in the street, kicked up a puff of dust, then careened away.

"I could've killed you then, if I'd wanted to," Shardeen yelled.

"I know you could've," Lance shouted back. "I appreciate that you didn't."

"I want something for it."

"What do you want? Maybe we can work something out."

"I need a horse."

"Let the girl go."

"The horse first, then I let her go."

Buck listened to the bartering as he hurried through the gully to the back of the barbershop. When he reached the end of the gully, he raised up to look over the edge, and saw a growth of low mesquite halfway between the barbershop and the Malone house. He knew that he could be seen if Shardeen happened to glance through the side window, but he had no choice. He had to try and move closer.

Buck ran in one quick movement to the mesquite trees, then he dived to the ground and scooted under the branches. From here he was only seventy-five feet away.

"I'm gettin' tired of talkin'!" Shardeen shouted. His voice sounded very close now.

"Let us see the girl!" Lance called.

"What for?"

"I want to see that she's not hurt!"

"She's not hurt!" Shardeen called back. "I'll put her in the window, but I'm holdin' my gun on her."

That was good. Buck knew that if Shardeen was going to be in the front window, it would give him a chance to make the dash across open ground, unobserved.

"All right, here she is!" Shardeen called.

Buck got up and ran hard, toward the side of the house. He reached it in a couple of seconds, then leaned back against the brick wall, gasping hard for breath. This wouldn't do. He would have to get his breath back before he sneaked into the house, else Shardeen would hear him.

"You seen her!" Shardeen called. "Now what's keepin' you?"

"We're talking it over!" Lance called back.

"Talkin' it over? What do you mean, you're talkin' it over? Listen to me! You ain't got no one to talk it over with but me. If I don't see a fresh horse in the street in one minute, I'm goin' to kill this girl."

"All right, all right, we'll do it," Lance answered. "We've just got to find a horse, that's all."

Buck tried the back door but it was locked and he knew he couldn't break through it without being heard. He tried two or three of the ground-level windows and discovered the same thing. He was getting frustrated, when he happened to notice that one of the windows on the second floor was open about six inches. The only problem was how to get up there. Then Buck looked at the comer of the house and saw a way up. He moved down to the corner, grabbed hold of the rainspout, and began climbing up to the second story. Once he reached the second story he stepped over onto the mansard, the little skirt of a roof that completely surrounded the house at that level.

Buck worked his way carefully down the side of the house until he reached the window. Then he raised if slowly, quietly, and stepped inside.

"I ain't goin' to wait much longer!" Shardeen shouted, and Buck jumped, for the voice was from the very next room.

Buck entered the house through one of the bedrooms. He pulled his pistol then walked across the floor as quietly as he could, then opened the door to peek out into the hall. He got a sudden start, for there, right in front of him, he saw Shardeen and Lucinda. Then he realized that he wasn't actually seeing them. What he was seeing was their reflection. A full-length mirror hung in the hall just across from the room where Shardeen was holed up. Buck could see Shardeen and Lucinda standing by the front window. He realized then that he could use the mirror to see where Shardeen was at all times. He could also gauge where Lucinda was, and thus avoid hitting her if he had to shoot. He took a cautious step forward, then cringed, because the floor creaked loudly under his weight.

"Who's there?" Shardeen said, spinning around quickly.

When Shardeen turned around, he saw the full figure of Buck Chaney coming toward him with his gun drawn. Shardeen fired instantly...and the mirror shattered into pieces.

"What the hell?" Shardeen shouted, not realizing he had just shot at Buck's image.

The moment Shardeen discovered his presence, Buck dived to the floor, then rolled over in front of the door with his gun pointing up. Shardeen, who was still confused by the mirror, didn't see Buck until it was too late. Buck fired once, and his bullet caught Shardeen under the chin, then exited through the top rear of his head, carrying with its egress, a pink mist of blood. Shardeen fell back, then crashed through the window.

Lucinda screamed and Buck jumped to his feet, quickly.

"Are you all right?" Buck asked.

"Oh, Buck!" she said, running to him. He took her in his arms. "I was so frightened!"

"Buck! Buck, are you up there?" Lance called from down in the street.

Buck moved to the front window and looked down. Shardeen lay sprawled on his back in the street below. His eyes were open and sightless and his gun lay in the dirt beside him. All the curious of the town were beginning to gather around his body.

"I'm here, Lance," Buck called down.

"Come on down here, little brother. We're going after the Beekmans."

CHAPTER 13

A HOT DRY WIND MOVED THROUGH THE canyon, pushing before it a billowing puff of red dust. The cloud of dust lifted high and spread out wide, making it look as if there were blood on the sun.

Lance and Buck had ridden into the canyon and now Buck was squatting on the sunbaked ground, holding the reins of his horse and reading a sign which told him that two other riders had come here before them.

"It looks like they came this way," he said. "Both of them."

"They're not carrying any extra weight," Lance offered.

"No, they're not," Buck replied. He sighed. "I guess maybe Armstrong was right. There was no gold. It's just as well, I suppose. I sure wasn't going to watch you turn it back in."

"And I wasn't going to let you keep it."

"How were you going to stop me?" Buck asked. Something caught Lance's attention and he twisted in his saddle to look up toward the high denuded wall of the red mesa which boxed in the canyon. He saw a flash of light, like the sun's reflection off the, polished barrel of a Henry.

"Fortunately, it looks like we'll never have to settle that question," Lance said. He pointed. "They're up there, Buck."

Buck stood and looked a quarter of the way up the canyon wall. There was another flash, only this time it wasn't the sun, it was a tiny wink of fire. They heard the rifle's report an instant before the bullet hit a rock nearby, then whined as it ricocheted away. A little cloud of smoke drifted away from the rifle.

"That's them," Buck said. He pulled his rifle from its scabbard. Lance climbed down from his horse with his own rifle in hand.

"There's only one way we're going to get them out of there," Lance said to his brother.

"I know," Buck answered. "We're going to have to go after them."

Buck took the canteen off his saddle pommel, then dropped the reins and slapped his horse to send him out of the line of fire. Lance did the same thing with his animal.

"We've been in these situations before, little brother," Lance said.

"Yeah," Buck answered, flashing a big smile. "At least this time we're on the same side."

"One of us needs to get to those rocks over there," Lance said, pointing to a collection of boulders which were located near the base of the cliff.

"One of us? Which one of us?"

"You're the youngest and the fastest," Lance said. "Anyway, I'll cover you."

Buck sighed. "I was afraid you'd say that." He took a deep breath, then started running toward the rocks Lance had pointed out. Lance began firing up toward the canyon wall, but that didn't prevent the Beekmans from shooting back. Buck saw puffs of dust and heard the bullets whining as they came near him. Finally, with a dive which covered the last five yards, he made it to the rocks.

"All right, Lance," he called. "It's your turn." Buck began firing to cover Lance's dash, and because he was in a better position to provide covering fire than Lance had been, his covering fire was so effective that the Beekmans weren't able to get off one shot.

"I don't know what you were so afraid of," Lance said a moment later as, panting for breath, he dropped down beside his brother. "I thought that was pretty easy."

"Sure. It was a Sunday stroll," Buck agreed. He stared up toward the Beekmans. "Now what?"

Lance raised up and looked around, then he saw a possible way up the side of the canyon wall. He followed it with his eyes and saw that it led to a shelf which overlooked the spot where the Beekmans had taken cover. It was evident that the Beekmans hadn't noticed it, or they wouldn't have taken the position they had.

"Look up there," Lance said, pointing to the trail. "If we could get up there, we'd have a clear shot at them."

"Yeah," Buck said. "How could they have missed that?"

"Because they rode on through the canyon, then came back to set up an ambush," Lance said. "They must've come down from the top. Come on, let's go-

Though the route they selected had looked passable from the ground, climbing it proved to be very difficult. When Buck and Lance had been at it for roughly half-an-hour, it didn't seem as if they had gained so much as an inch. However, when they looked back toward the ground, they could see that they were making progress, for by now they were dangerously high.

With Lance in the lead, they clung to the side of the mountain and moved only when they had a secure handhold or foothold...tiny though it might be. Sweat poured into their eyes and they grew thirsty with their effort, but still they climbed. Suddenly Lance stopped.

"What is it?" Buck asked. "Why did you stop?"

"I'm not sure we can go on here," Lance replied. "We've got no choice."

"There's no place to get a hold."

"There's bound to be some place," Buck said. "Keep looking."

"There's nothing," Lance said. "We've got to backtrack a little ways, maybe go up that other chute over there."

"Damn," Buck swore. "All right, come on back, we'll try it."

"Where'd they go?" Carl asked, peering over the rock to look down toward where he had last seen the Chaney brothers.

"I don't know," Clay answered. He inched forward on his stomach, and as he did so, he dislodged several rocks which tumbled over the edge then echoed loudly as they clattered and bounced all the way down to the canyon floor.

"Do you see them?"

"No."

"Son of a bitch! What happened to them?"

"I don't know," Clay said again. He eased his way back from the edge of the shelf, then twisted around to face his brother. "Listen, I'm for gettin' the hell out of here," he said.

"And just leave them to come after us?"

"No, not that. But we need to find another position. If we stay here and they manage to work their way up to the top, we're goin' to be sittin' ducks. And don't forget, we still got Shardeen to worry about. He's not goin' to believe there wasn't no gold."

"Shardeen's dead," Carl said with conviction. "What makes you think that?"

"Because it's the Chaneys who have come after us. Do you think they'd be down there now if Shardeen was still alive?"

"I don't know," Clay answered. "Maybe not. But if he is dead, then that means they killed him, and in my book that makes them more dangerous than he was. I don't aim to stay around and let them sneak up on me. Come on, let's get out of here."

Clay started back up the path that led to the top of the cliff, and Carl followed.

"Lance, wait, listen!" Buck hissed, and Lance stopped. They were both still for a moment, then they heard the sound of small rocks being dislodged and falling to the canyon floor below. "Do you hear it?"

"Yes," Lance answered. "What is that?"

"They're moving!" Buck said. "Damn, they're climbing back to the top. They're trying to get away!"

"Yeah? Well, they're not going to make it," Lance said, and he reached for another rock to improve his position.

Even though they had changed routes, it was still very difficult going. In front of them was nothing but the sheer rock face of the cliff. Behind them was thin air, and below them, a sheer drop of over three hundred feet to the rocky canyon floor.

When they changed routes, Buck had assumed the lead and now it was he who found the hand-holds and tiny crevices. Sweat poured into his eyes as he climbed, but he could think of nothing except the Beekmans, and the picture of his sister lying there, dead and molested by those animals. He reached for a small slate outcropping, but as he put his weight on it, it failed. With a sickening sensation in his stomach, he felt himself falling.

Lance was just beneath his brother and when he heard the slate crack, he looked up, just as Buck started to fall. Lance was in a good position, due to his grip of a sturdy juniper tree. He held onto the tree with one hand, and with the other reached out and grabbed Buck, just as Buck slid by. He slammed Buck against the wall and Buck, feeling the rocks scrape and tear at his flesh, flailed against the wall with his hands until he managed to get a hold.

"I've got it," he said to Lance, and Lance, whose own grip was loosening, let go of Buck so he could improve his position.

"Thanks," Buck said, as he leaned against the wall, breathing hard,

"Are you all right?"

"Yeah," Buck said. He took a deep breath. "Come on, let's go. We can't stay here all day, those bastards will get away."

Buck and Lance started climbing again.

After two more minutes of climbing it began to get a little easier, then easier still, until finally they reached a ledge which showed signs of having been a trail at one time, possibly a trail which had existed until erosion took part of it away. They even found that they could walk upright, and, shortly after that, they made it to the top.

"Where do you think they are?" Buck heard Carl say. Buck held up his hand in a signal for Lance to be quiet.

"How the hell am I supposed to know?" Clay answered irritably. "Just keep lookin' for them."

The Beekmans were no more than twenty-five yards away from them, peering down toward the canyon floor, totally unaware that Buck and Lance had also reached the top.

"You don't have to look all that hard, boys," Buck said. "We're right over here."

"What the hell?" Clay gasped. "How'd you two get up here? They ain't no way a mountain goat could'a come up, except the way we took."

"Maybe we're part mountain goat," Lance suggested.

"Maybe you are at that," Clay agreed. He grinned. "You sure as hell smell like one."

The four men stood on top of the mesa, silhouetted against the brilliant blue sky. All four had their guns holstered, and for a moment they formed an eerie tableau, a moment frozen in eternity.

"Let's do it," Clay said, and, so saying, his hand went for his gun.

Clay's gun didn't even break leather before Buck's gun was out and booming. Carl's gun and Lance's fired at about the same time, but Lance's bullet found a target while Carl's shot whistled harmlessly between Buck and Lance.

Buck's shot hit Clay between the eyes and he fell back with blood, brain-matter, and little pieces of bone splattering out of the hole made by the bullet's exit wound. Carl was hit in the chest and he stood there for a moment, looking on in total surprise. He tried to take a step forward, lost his balance, then fell. Lance and Buck went over to him and looked down at him.

"You boys have wasted your bullets and your time," Carl gasped. "There ain't no gold."

"This wasn't for the gold," Lance said. "This was for Becky."

"Becky?"

"Don't tell me you don't know who she is," Buck said angrily.

Carl chuckled. "Oh, you mean the girl at the farm. Well, we never exactly got on a first name basis."

"You bastard."

"Was she your sister?"

"Yes."

Carl had been clutching his hand over his wound and he pulled it away now and looked at the blood that had pooled in the palm of his hand. "Oh, that hurts," he said. "Son of a bitch that hurts." He looked up at Buck and Lance. "Your sister, you say? Well, she wasn't all that good. I've had better."

Buck cocked his pistol and pointed it at Carl's head.

"Buck, no!" Lance said. "Can't you see what he's doing?"

Buck looked around, questioningly.

"He's trying to get you to make his dying easier," Lance said, coldly.

"Yeah," Buck said. He sighed and let the hammer back down slowly. "Yeah, I guess you're right. This way it could take him a day...maybe two, to die. Come on, let's get out of here."

"No!" Carl shouted. "No, you aren't goin' to leave me like this!" He tried to stand up, but the pain was too great and he fell back again. When he fell, he fell on a gun, either his or Clay's. He picked it up.

"You bastards!" he gurgled.

Lance looked around just as Carl started to pick up the gun.

"Buck, look out!" he called, shoving his brother out of the line of fire as he started for his own gun.

Carl raised the pistol but, to Lance's surprise, he didn't aim it at either of them. Instead, he put the barrel to his temple, then, with an insane grin, he pulled the trigger.

Both Buck and Lance stood in momentary shock as the echo of the shot rolled back from the canyon below, its reverberating sound living longer than Carl Beekman. After that there was absolute silence.

"Come on," Lance said. "It's a long way back to our horses."

"What about them?"

Lance looked back toward the two dead Beekmans. When he looked up, he saw a pair of buzzards, already drawn by the smell of fresh blood.

"Don't worry about them," he said. "They'll be taken care of."

A LOOK AT BOOK 2: THE CHANEY EDGE

It Takes Two Loyal Brothers to Outsmart a Texas Outlaw.

Buck Chaney first crosses paths with Rufus Blanton on a West Texas train car halted suddenly in the night. Rufus is on board-and set on robbing every passenger. When a shootout with Buck leaves two of his gunmen dead, the outlaw gets away with his life - but without any loot. He'll come back to haunt Buck Chaney and his brother Lance.

AVAILABLE NOW

ABOUT THE AUTHOR

Robert Vaughan sold his first book when he was 19. That was 57 years and nearly 500 books ago. Vaughan wrote, produced, and appeared in the History Channel documentary Vietnam Homecoming. His books have hit the NYT bestseller list seven times. He has won the Spur Award, the PORGIE Award (Best Paperback Original), the Western Fictioneers Lifetime Achievement Award, received the Readwest President's Award for Excellence in Western Fiction, is a member of the American Writers Hall of Fame and is a Pulitzer Prize nominee. Vaughn is also a retired army officer, helicopter pilot with three tours in Vietnam. And received the Distinguished Flying Cross, the Purple Heart, The Bronze Star with three oak leaf clusters, the Air Medal for valor with 35 oak leaf clusters, the Army Commendation Medal, the Meritorious Service Medal, and the Vietnamese Cross of Gallantry.

Made in the USA
Middletown, DE
05 September 2019